No. K210292

Date of Return	Date of Return

WITHDRAWN

WITHDRAWN

RED IS THE VALLEY

When the showdown set in between the Cattlemen's Association and the farmers of the Valley, rancher Jim Baron stood in the middle, taking sides with neither group. On the surface the conflict appeared to be the traditional struggle between ranchers and farmers; this time rustling was the problem and the farmers were the accused.

As tempers grew short and passions flared up, Jim knew he could no longer hold himself back. He had to act, though in doing so he antagonized everyone as he discovered the real core of the clash. Two determined antagonists—one a rancher, the other a farmer—were bent on gaining sole control of the entire valley, and had vowed to stop at nothing to do it. Jim Baron rode alone—and his life and the future of that Wyoming land were at stake.

Joseph Wayne was a pseudonym used by Wayne D. Overholser, an author who has won three Golden Spur awards from the Western Writers of America and who has a long list of fine Western titles to his credit. Overholser was born in Pomeroy, Washington, and attended the University of Montana, University of Oregon, and the University of Southern California before becoming a public school teacher and principal in various Oregon communities. He began writing for Western pulp magazines in 1936 and within a couple of years was a regular contributor to Street & Smith's *Western Story Magazine* and Fiction House's *Lariat Story Magazine*. *Buckaroo's Code* (1947) was his first Western novel and remains one of his best. In the 1950s and 1960s, having retired from academic work to concentrate on writing, he would publish as many as four books a year under his own name or a pseudonym, most prominently as Joseph Wayne. *The Violent Land* (1954), *The Lone Deputy* (1957), and *The Bitter Night* (1961) are among the finest of his early Overholser titles. Overholser's Western novels are based on a solid knowledge of the history and customs of the 19th-Century West, particularly when set in his two favorite Western states, Oregon and Colorado. Many of his novels are first person narratives, a technique that tends to bring an added dimension of vividness to the frontier experiences of his narrators and frequently, as in *Cast a Long Shadow* (1957), the female characters one encounters are among the most memorable. He has written his numerous novels with a consistent skill and an uncommon sensitivity to the depths of human character. Almost invariably, his stories weave a spell of their own with their scenes and images of social and economic forces often in conflict and the diverse ways of life and personalities that made the American Western frontier so unique a time and place in human history. *Nugget City* (1997) *Riders Of The Sundowns* (1997) and *Chumley's Gold* (1998) are his latest books.

RED IS THE VALLEY

Joseph Wayne

GUNSMOKE

First published in the U.K. by Gold Lion Books

This hardback edition 2002
by Chivers Press
by arrangement with
Golden West Literary Agency

ISBN 0 7540 8184 2

British Library Cataloguing in Publication Data available.

Printed and bound in Great Britain by
BOOKCRAFT, Midsomer Norton, Somerset

1

Jim Baron was repairing the corral gate when his sister Rose cried out, "Jim, look." He wheeled toward the house. Rose was pointing to the ridge to the south that lay between the forks of the Slow Water. Sam Clegg was riding toward the Baron place, three other riders out behind him.

Jim tossed his hammer into the nail bucket and ran to the house. When he reached the porch, Rose asked anxiously, "What are you going to do?"

"Get my gun," he said. "What else can I do?"

She grabbed his arm. "No. You'll just make trouble. Do what he tells you."

"Like Pa always did?" Jim shook his head. "Not me. This has been coming ever since Pa died. I'm not going to duck it now that it finally got here."

He jerked free from her grasp and went into the house. He heard her cry, "You've got to be practical, Jim. You can't . . . You can't . . ."

He didn't pause to hear the rest of it. He went on into his bedroom, yanked open the top drawer of the bureau, and took out his gun belt. His mother had died when he was a baby, and Rose, who was twenty years older than he was, had raised him and kept house for him and his father. He was very much aware that he owed her a great deal, but that did not include obedience, not at this stage of the game.

Rose was still on the porch when he left the house. She gripped his arm again, her face pale, the corners of her mouth trembling. "Jim, what's going to happen to me if they kill you? Have you thought of that?"

He looked down at her and nodded. She was forty-three, an old maid who would never marry, a tall, skinny woman who reminded him almost every day that she had given up everything for him and their father, and that after their father had died last year, she was doing the same for Jim.

She loved her misery, he told himself; she would not be happy if she weren't miserable. He was sure the thought had never occurred to her that both of them would be better off if she'd just go away and stop sacrificing for him.

"Sam won't kill me," Jim said, and jerked free again from her grip. "But maybe you had better go inside."

"Have you forgotten Carrie?" Rose demanded. "You can never bring her here if you kill her father."

He strode across the yard, thinking that regardless of whatever trouble he had with Carrie's father, he could not marry her and bring her to the B-in-a-Box as long as Rose remained at home, and Rose showed no intention of leaving. He couldn't build a house big enough for the two women, and no one knew it better than he did.

When he reached the corral, he checked his gun and eased it back into leather. He didn't expect trouble, but if it came, he'd knock Sam Clegg out of his saddle before they cut him down. He was sure Sam knew it, and that was the best guarantee he could have that there would not be any trouble today.

They came on down off the ridge and across the grass, riding easily, Clegg holding his position in front as he always did so that no one could possibly mistake his relationship with the men who worked for him. He was a big man about fifty, with a bald head, a neck as solid as an oak corner post, and tremendous shoulders. He was an arrogant man who had always given orders and had never taken them as long as Jim could remember, so trouble between them had been inevitable from the day Hank Baron, Jim's father, had died.

Sam reined up twenty feet from Jim and signaled his men to stop. Jim did not know them, but that proved nothing. Clegg's outfit, Skull, was by far the biggest in the county, employing twenty or more riders. Clegg was a hard man to work for, so there was always considerable turnover.

Clegg gave Jim his arrogant half-inch nod, and Jim nodded back in the same manner. Clegg cleared his throat. He said, "I've been aiming to come over for several days, Jim, but hadn't got around to it. We're having a meeting of the Slow Water Cattlemen's Association at my place tonight. Of course we wanted you to know."

"Thanks, Sam," Jim said.

"You coming?"

"I dunno."

Clegg shifted his weight in the saddle and scowled. He said, "We've been sitting on our fat butts too long, Jim. I lost at least a hundred head of steers this winter and I've talked to all the other cattlemen except you. They've had considerable loss, more than a mild winter and predatory animals could account for. As you know, the sheriff's office does nothing. How many have you lost?"

"No more than usual," Jim answered. "Three or four."

Clegg shrugged. "The rest of us have lost so many we can't go on overlooking what's happening." He motioned downstream. "I'm on my way to warn every thieving bastard on the Slow Water that he's gonna have to get out. We've been patient too long and the rustlers are getting more daring all the time."

To Sam Clegg, as with many cowmen, the word settler and rustler were synonymous. As far as Jim knew, none of the settlers on the Slow Water had ever stolen any steers, but Clegg had been accusing them of it ever since the first homesteader had staked out his claim which had been three years ago. Now he apparently had persuaded his neighbors to back him, all but Jim Baron.

"Sam, it ain't no surprise to you, I reckon," Jim said, "but I don't want no part of this. If you can prove this rustling talk, the sheriff will have to do something. If you can't these people have a right to live on land that they settled and filed on, legal and proper."

"That's the real reason I'm here." Clegg leaned forward in the saddle. "You belong to the Cattlemen's Association.

Your pa was one of the founders. We have always accepted majority rule. Tonight we vote on the steps we're going to take to handle this situation. Now you'll either go along with the majority or you're with the rustlers. If that's the case, by God we'll make this country too hot to hold you."

"Then you'd better start heating the country up, Sam," Jim said. "I sure ain't going along with no trumped-up charge against these people."

Clegg sucked in a long breath and blew it out. "I'm sorry you said that, boy. Your pa and me were friends. We settled on the Slow Water when the Cheyenne and Sioux were raiding through here. We fought 'em. We fought outlaws. I helped send your pa to the legislature." He shook his head. "You always were a stubborn whelp. If Hank had taken a blacksnake to you when you were a little shaver, you'd have growed up different."

"I reckon I would," Jim agreed, "but Pa wasn't that kind of a father."

For a moment Clegg was silent, his pale blue eyes locked with Jim's, then he asked, "You claim these people as friends? Is that why you're backing them instead of the Association?"

"Some are my friends," Jim said. "Some ain't. No, that's not the reason."

"All right," Clegg said. "I guess you know how it stacks up. By evening every rustler on the Slow Water will be warned to get out of the country. One more thing. Stay away from Carrie. I've told you before. I won't tell you again."

Clegg jerked his head at the others and rode downstream. The three cowhands grinned knowingly like three lackeys who were paid to follow along and not have a thought of their own. Jim stood motionless watching them as they rode away. He doubted that Clegg believed his own talk about rustling. It was just an excuse, but why, after all these months, was he actually making his move?

Jim saddled his buckskin, finding no answer to his question. As he mounted, Rose hurried across the yard to him. She said, "I thought you'd come and tell me what happened."

"Nothing more than you could guess," Jim said. "He's fixing to run the settlers off the Slow Water. Says they're rustlers and I'm supposed to go to a meeting of the Cattlemen's Association tonight."

"You're going, of course," she said.

"No, I'm not going," he said sharply. "Nothing is really important to Sam Clegg except having his own way. He ain't gonna have it with me. If I did go, they'd outvote me. He's got the others in the Association lined up, or he wouldn't have come here to tell me about the meeting."

"Oh Jim," she said. "Why do you have to be such a fool? Pa always got along with him. So can you."

"I'll be back in time for supper," he said curtly, and turned the buckskin upstream into the mountains.

He knew it was true that his father had always got along with Sam Clegg, but only because he never opposed anything Clegg wanted. That was why the Cattlemen's Association had been formed; it was the reason Hank Baron had gone to the legislature. He had never been his own man; he had never held his head up, and Jim knew he had despised himself.

Both Sam Clegg and Hank Baron had come to the Slow Water with shirttail outfits. Clegg had prospered, Hank hadn't and the reason had been simple enough. Clegg had no conscience, Hank had. Over the years the Skull herd had grown, the B-in-a-Box herd had not.

Jim had often asked himself whether the old adage about honesty being the best policy was true. True or not, he wouldn't, or couldn't, live the way Sam Clegg did. How Clegg had ever managed to raise a daughter like Carrie was more than Jim could understand.

The canyon walls of the North Fork closed in around him. The air grew cooler and sweeter as he climbed. Within half an hour he reached the waterfalls where he had been meeting Carrie every Saturday morning since the weather had turned warm. She thought her father didn't know she'd been seeing him, but she'd been dead wrong about that, he told himself. Maybe Clegg had put one of his men to trailing her.

Jim dismounted, loosened the cinch, and let the reins drag. He lay down and stared at the sky through the twinkling leaves of the quaking asps, wondering what he was going to do. As Rose had said, he wasn't practical. And Clegg had been right about one thing. He'd always been a stubborn whelp.

Well, he wasn't going to change. He didn't think he could. The hard fact was that, whether he changed or not, he or no other ten-cow rancher could buck Skull, let alone the entire Cattlemen's Association. As far as the settlers were concerned, they'd probably walk out just as Clegg told them to. Maybe Clegg was promoting this sudden push to get Jim out of the country. It struck him that he was going to end up dead either way he played it.

A moment later he heard Carrie riding down the south side of the canyon. He got up and waited for her. She was twenty, but she had been a grown woman from the time she'd been sixteen. She'd let Jim know even before that that she was in love with him.

At first Clegg had ignored it, thinking that in time they'd get tired of each other and drift apart, but when they'd gone to him asking permission to marry, he'd blown up and told Jim he'd have to own more than a poverty spread like the B-in-a-Box if he wanted to marry Sam Clegg's daughter.

After that they'd met secretly. Now, watching her as she rode down the steep slope and crossed the creek, he told himself glumly that they were going to have to stop seeing each other for a while.

She reined up and he gave her a hand. For a moment she stood looking up at him, a slender, blond girl who was, to Jim Baron, the most beautiful woman in the world. When he told her that, she always laughed and said he was prejudiced, and he had to admit that he was.

He swept her into his arms and kissed her, and when he let her go, she whispered, "I've only got a minute. He told me this morning that if I didn't quit seeing you, he'd have you beaten to death. I think he would, Jim. He's getting worse, Jim. I think he's crazy."

"He came by this morning," Jim said.

"He's called a meeting of the Cattlemen's Association and told you to come," she said. "That it?"

He nodded. "I'm not going."

"I knew you wouldn't," she said. "Did he tell you what they're planning?"

"Just that he's warning the settlers to get out."

"I've heard him talk to some of the others," she said. "I've spied on them and eavesdropped. I've had my ear to the keyhole most of the week. They're hiring an assassin. Somebody like Tom Horn. They figure that a couple of murders will be enough to send the settlers packing."

Horrified, Jim stared at her. "He wouldn't go that far."

"He would," she said, "and you're on the list. Jim, you've got to leave the country."

2

For a moment Jim stared at her, an all-gone feeling deep in his belly. She might as well have asked him to cut off a hand. He wheeled away from her and, hunkering beside the creek, started tossing rocks into the deep pool in front of him.

"I can't do that, Carrie," he said finally.

"Why?" She knelt beside him. "I'll go with you, Jim. I know we don't have any money, but we can work. I'm twenty years old. Pa can't make me stay home. He doesn't even have any right to tell me what to do." She dropped a hand on his arm. "Jim, I don't want you killed!"

"Why am I on the list?" he asked. "I'm not a settler."

"I don't know," she answered. "Maybe he thinks he can break us up. He tells me he has great plans for me, but he never tells me what they are."

"I guess he'll break us up if he kills me," Jim said.

"It's not funny," she said quickly. "We will have to quit seeing each other if you won't leave the country. I'd even marry somebody else if I was sure it would take you off Pa's list."

"Let's not go that far," he said.

"Jim, I don't think anybody understands Pa," she said. "Or that he understands himself. I guess that's why I worry about him doing something crazy. He's thought up all the usual reasons for wanting the settlers driven out. Like saying there's only a dozen families on the Slow Water now, but if they're allowed to stay, more will come and they'll have a majority in the country and they'll elect the county officials.

"The sheriff is the one he's anxious about. As long as he's got Buck Riley in office, he feels safe. If Riley was replaced by a man who was friendly to the settlers, he'd worry, and Pa doesn't like to worry."

She paused, studying the side of his face, then she went on, "Jim, sometimes I think he's afraid of you. He says you're tough and that people will listen to you and follow you. Nobody has ever openly defied Pa and he knows you will. Maybe that's the real reason you're on the list. Now will you leave the country? For a while anyway?"

He shook his head. "You know I won't, Carrie. In the first place, I can't. I'm not built that way. In the second place, I can't go off and leave the B-in-a-Box. Pa and me worked it together when he was alive. After he died, I've tried to keep it going by myself except for some help during haying. I've grown up on it and it's the only home I know. If I walked off and left it, I'd lose everything."

"And there's Rose," Carrie said bitterly. "I hate her, Jim. I know I shouldn't say that about your sister, but we both know that if everything else was fine and dandy, we still couldn't get married."

"That's right," Jim said. "She never comes out and says it, but in her own way she never lets me forget it."

He picked up another rock and tossed it into the pool. He couldn't tell Carrie, but he hated his sister as much as Carrie did. There simply was no solution to the problem. Rose was healthy enough to live another fifty years.

She had no other close relative. She had no place to go. More than that, she owned fifty percent of the B-in-a-Box, so she had as much right to live on it as he did. She would never admit it, but the truth was she had dedicated her life to taking care of Jim, and, in effect, to keeping Carrie from moving in with her and Jim.

"I've got to go," Carrie said. "I don't want to start anybody looking for me and making trouble for you." She hesitated, then asked softly, "You're sure you won't leave the country, not even if I go with you?"

"I'm sure."

"If anything changes your mind and you want me to go with you, get word to Nora Bain in town. She'll bring any message to me that you want to send."

She rose and walked to her horse. He followed and, putting his hands on her shoulders, turned her to face him. "No matter what happens between me and Sam, remember that I love you."

"I'll never forget it," she said.

They both knew this was good-bye for a while at least, perhaps for as long as Sam Clegg lived. He filled his eyes with the sight of her, the bright blue eyes, the hair that seemed so yellow when set against her sun-tanned skin, the pert nose.

Then he could not stand it any longer and he took her into his arms and held her, and for a moment the temptation to go away with her was very strong. He would be free, and as long as he stayed here, he would be in prison with no prospects of escape.

"I've got to go, Jim," she said, and lifted her mouth for his kiss.

He gave her a hand and she mounted and rode downstream. He stood watching until she crossed the creek and started angling up the south side of the canyon. Turning back to the water, he hunkered down on the bank and rolled and lighted a cigarette. He should go home. There was work to be done. It seemed that he was always behind. But he wasn't going back. Not yet. It had been hard to let her go. The work would still be there when he got home. Here at least a man could dream.

He listened to the pulsating pound of the water as it tumbled over the ledge above him and whirled and beat itself into foam, then swept on downstream, forming this deep, blue pool. There were always trout down there in the bottom, the big, wise ones who somehow managed to avoid being caught. They were smarter than he was, he thought sourly. He was caught and he didn't see any way out.

He heard a pair of pine squirrels chattering somewhere above him; he saw the blue flash of a jay as it darted through the timber below him. Somewhere back in the brush he heard the rustle of dried leaves as a chipmunk raced from one tree to another. These were the sounds and the movements of life, and for this moment he felt a deep and abiding peace, and then, suddenly, it was shattered.

"On your feet bucko," a man said from somewhere behind him. "Keep your hand away from your gun."

He rose and made a slow turn. Three men stood at the edge of the brush, one with a gun in his hand. He knew all of them, Skull riders who had worked for Sam Clegg for years. The man with the gun was Dutch Manders. The other two were Chick Lund and Bones Porter.

Some of the Skull hands were like the three men who had followed Sam Clegg that morning, transients who worked a while and would probably drift on, but the others were like these three, men who drew fighting wages and fitted perfectly into Clegg's way of doing things. Jim knew he was in for it. They had come to do a job and they'd do it or kill him.

"Good," Manders said. "Now unbuckle your gun belt and let it drop."

Jim hesitated, his eyes searching Mander's face. No use to buck him. Manders would kill him and tie his body on the buckskin and take him to town and turn him over to Buck Riley with a cock-and-bull story that would account for his murder and Riley would accept it. That would be the end of the whole business.

So Jim obeyed again. Manders said, "Pick up the gun belt, Chick. Toss it over yonder. Just get it out of reach for a while."

Chick Lund stepped forward, picked up the gun belt and threw it to the other side of the clearing. Then Mandars said, "We followed Miss Carrie. The boss told her to stay away from you and he made it clear what would happen if she didn't. We didn't want to get her all worked up, so we waited until she left. All right, Chick, go to work on him."

The gun in Manders' hand was lined on Jim's belt buckle. The hammer was back. It would take only a slight pressure by Manders' trigger finger and there would be a chunk of lead in Jim's belly.

"Carrie asked me to leave the country," Jim said.

Lund had moved behind Jim and now grabbed his wrists and yanked them behind his back. Manders said, "If you're gonna pull your freight, we won't lay a hand on you. Sam would like nothing better than for you to get out of the country. You'll be a damned trouble maker as long as you're here, but it's my guess you're stupid enough to stay and keep on making trouble."

"Yeah, I guess I'm stupid," Jim said.

Porter moved up. He was a big man, the strongest of the three and without the streak of brutality that characterized the other two. He said apologetically, "Nothing personal in this, Jim. I'm glad you didn't jump the gun and start a fight. Dutch wants to kill you. He says that's the only way to teach trouble makers a lesson, but I figure you'll catch on and dog it out of the country after I get done."

Jim sagged in Lund's grip and lashed out with both feet, his boots catching the big man in the belly and knocking him back on his heels. Lund let go and Jim fell flat on his back. Manders fired, the bullet kicking up dirt inches from Jim's head.

"You see, Bones?" Manders said. "He's a stupid bastard like I said. He can't learn."

"Don't kill him," Porter said.

Jim rolled over and got to his hands and knees just as Lund kicked him in the ribs, knocking wind out of him and dropping him flat on his belly again. Lund yanked him to his feet and whirled him around so that he faced Bones Porter.

Porter hit him on the side of the head, knocking him back into Lund's arms. Lund pushed him forward and Porter hit him again, rocking his head and sending the earth into a tilted spin. Lund let him fall.

"That's enough," Porter said.

"Oh hell, Dutch," Lund said. "Let him have it in the guts. I tell you he'll make us sorry if we don't beef him."

"No," Porter said. "Sam told us to rough him up. If he

ain't out of the country in a day or two, we will beef him. Let's ride."

Jim didn't lose consciousness, but he came close. He heard, he could see in a strange, distorted way, but he couldn't move. Now, with the seconds ticking away, he thought Dutch Manders was going to do what Chick Lund said. Lund was right. If he lived, he'd make them sorry for what they had done this morning.

"All right," Manders said after a long pause. "We'll ride, but if there is a next time, it will be the end of one tough bucko named Jim Baron."

He holstered his gun and wheeled and walked upslope to the horses. Lund followed, but Bones Porter lingered for a few seconds, staring at Jim. He said, "You're a good fighting man, Baron, but you can't win. All Sam wants is to get you off his back. You'd better slope out and live. There just ain't no percentage in dying at your age."

Then Porter followed the other two. Jim didn't move. He stared at the sky through the twisting, dancing leaves of the quaking asps. He hurt, his thoughts were wild and distorted, but he knew one thing for a certainty. They should have killed him if they wanted to live.

3

Jim lay there a long time, or what seemed a long time before he found the strength to crawl to the creek and slosh the cold water over his bruised face. He hurt whenever he took a deep breath, so he guessed he had some broken ribs, but he didn't think any of the bones of his face were broken and he was thankful for that.

Carrie wanted him to leave because he was on her father's list; Bones Porter figured that he'd dog it out of the country after taking a beating. Well, they were both wrong, he told himself as he crawled to the other side of the clearing where Chick Lund had tossed his gun belt. Carrie wanted to keep him alive. Maybe he wouldn't be when this was over, but either way, he aimed to show Porter he was wrong.

He got to his feet, moving slowly and carefully because he didn't know how badly he was hurt. He buckled his gun belt around his waist and walked to his horse. For a time he stood there, one hand on the horn, then he pulled himself into the saddle and sat there until the waves of pain began to die.

Jim rode downstream, his side still giving him stabs of agony every time the horse put a hoof down. By the time he reached the mouth of the canyon, the pain seemed to have lessened, but he wasn't sure that it actually had. Maybe he was numb.

He swung south, and presently came out on top of the ridge between the forks of the Slow Water. From here he could see the buildings of the B-in-a-Box and farther downstream the cabin that belonged to Ed Majors, the only real friend he could claim among the homesteaders.

Funny, he thought, how that after living here all these years, he had so few friends. But he knew the answer well enough. All of the settlers except Ed Majors distrusted him because he was a cowman, and the other cowmen took their cue from Sam Clegg who had made it a point to ostracize him from the moment he had asked permission to marry Carrie.

He had friends in town, Doc Ashton and Larry Bain, who owned the Mercantile, and the sheriff, Buck Riley. There were others, too, men who had known him all his life and had respected his father.

Still, it irritated him that the men he used to consider his friends, men who were in the same business he was, now treated him as if he were a pariah simply because they didn't have the guts it took to stand up to Sam Clegg.

He rode into Wheatridge, the county seat, early in the afternoon. He hadn't had dinner, but he couldn't eat the way he felt. Reining up in front of Doc Ashton's house at the west end of the business block, he eased out of the saddle, tied, and went in. The room to the right of the hall was the doctor's office. A sign on the desk read RING FOR THE DOCTOR. Jim tapped the bell and sat down.

Ashton came in a moment later. He said, "Howdy, Jim," took another look, and asked, "A grizzly?"

"Three Skull hands," Jim answered. "I can take one at a time, but not three, especially when Dutch Manders holds a gun on me."

Ashton was a young man, thirty or so, Jim judged, though he had never heard him give his age. He looked older because he was bald except for a circle of very light-colored hair. Oddly enough, he had bushy black brows and a heavy black mustache and beard. He had moved to Wheatridge as soon at he finished medical school, and had added to his education immediately by the practical training he received from digging bullets out of cowboys and setting broken bones and delivering babies.

For a moment Ashton stood looking down at Jim as he rubbed his bald head. He hated Sam Clegg and made no secret of the fact, or that he had little use for Clegg's way of doing things.

He'd gone to Skull several times during the winter when Clegg had been down in bed with chills and fever; he'd talked plain enough to Clegg about law and order, and what was going to happen if things weren't changed so that every man had equal rights in the county.

All he did was to relieve his feelings. He didn't change Clegg and he didn't change the way things were run. He was probably the only man in the county who could say what he had. Clegg knew he might need a doctor again someday, and Ashton was the only one in the county.

"How long, Jim?" Ashton demanded. "How much longer can Clegg and his plug uglies do just what they want to? How much longer can they go on disregarding the law and the rights of other people?"

"I don't know," Jim said. "All I know is that my side hurts like hell. How about looking me over?"

"All right," Ashton said. "Come back here into the other room and take your shirt off."

Ten minutes later Ashton said, "Doesn't look to me like you've got any broken bones, but that's an ugly bruise on your side. It'll be a few days before those muscles heal. Meanwhile don't do anything to strain them."

"I've got things to do whether I feel like it or not," Jim said. "Rose wants me to go along with Clegg the way Pa did. Carrie thinks I'll get killed if I don't pull my freight. Bones Porter figured I'd dog it out of the country after taking the beating I did."

"None of them know you very well, do they?" the doctor said. "Not even your sister or the girl you're going to marry."

"No, they don't," Jim said. "I guess women figure the worst thing that can happen to a man is to get killed, and Bones Porter judges everybody else by himself."

"He's right as far as most men are concerned," Ashton said. "I played poker with Buck Riley and Larry Bain and a few others last night. We talked about Clegg and how he's got everybody lined up his way, even here in town. The bank. The Mercantile. The livery stable. The newspaper. None of the businessmen want to rock the boat, so nobody's willing to buck Clegg but you'n me. Have you seen Riley yet?"

"No," Jim answered. "I'm going to the courthouse from here."

"Go ahead," Ashton said, "but it won't do you any good. From the talk last night, I got the idea that things will get worse before they get better. I mean, sooner or later Clegg will go too far and folks will rebel. I don't know when that'll be or what it'll take, but it's bound to happen."

"Murder," Jim said. "He's already warned the settlers to get out of the country. If they don't go, there will be some murders."

"He won't go that far." Ashton scratched the back of his neck, and then he said, "You know, by God, he might!"

"I don't know as to that." Jim shrugged. "Sam came by this morning to tell me he's having a meeting of the Cattlemen's Association at Skull tonight. I haven't made up my mind whether I oughtta go or not."

Ashton odded absent-mindedly. "You know, if Clegg is crazy, maybe we could get him committed. That'd fix things in a hurry."

"Now you're crazy," Jim said. "You'd never manage it."

"No. I guess not," Ashton said with regret. "Being crazy is a relative proposition. We're all a little crazy. Clegg is crazier'n the rest of us. The question is how crazy a man has to be before you can commit him. Does he have to commit murder?"

The whole proposition was stupid in Jim's opinion because Sam Clegg couldn't be touched even if he was half crazy. He asked, "How about the settlers? You know all of 'em pretty well. Will they move out like Sam ordered 'em to do?"

"No," Ashton said. "They'll fight. That's where Clegg is making his biggest mistake. You know Jeremy White? Lives downstream from you a couple of miles."

"I know who he is when I see him."

"Well, he's the one who'll get 'em to stand and fight. He's just as mean as Clegg and maybe even crazier."

"We'll soon know," Jim said.

As he left the doctor's office, he wondered how Jeremy White or anybody else could be as mean or as crazy as Sam Clegg.

4

Jim decided it was easier to walk to the courthouse than it was to pull himself into the saddle and ride one block and then dismount, so he left his buckskin tied in front of the doctor's office and walked slowly past the livery stable and the hotel and the Mercantile. When he reached the Palace, he saw three Skull horses racked in front. One of them was Dutch Manders' blue roan.

Jim paused, strongly tempted to go in and face Manders, but then went on to the courthouse, a frame building set in the center of the next block. It had needed paint for years, the yard had grown up in weeds, and if the structure simply collapsed because of neglect, no one in Slow Water would give a damn until it cost them tax money to build a new one.

The attitude was indicative of the way people felt about the law, and perhaps stemmed from Sam Clegg's feeling that if anything was done about a situation, he'd have to do it because the law wouldn't. If the old cliché about the government which governed the least was the best government, then Slow Water County had an excellent government.

Jim mounted the spur-scarred steps and crossed the hall to the sheriff's office. The jail was just beyond the office, one large cell where Buck Riley lodged the drunks until they sobered up, and two small cells across the corridor for those who committed major crimes. Jim could not remember when either of the small cells had been occupied.

Buck Riley sat at his desk, making a great pretense of being busy with paperwork. Jim dropped into a rawhide-bottom chair and canted it back against the wall and rolled and lighted a cigarette. He waited until Riley got around to looking up to see who had come in.

"Howdy, Jim," Riley said. "I didn't know who it was." He saw the purple bruises on Jim's face, and asked, "What happened?"

"That's why I'm here," Jim said, "but I was thinking as I sat here watching you that you're always busy when anybody comes in except Sam Clegg. Then the notion that you can recognize Sam's footsteps entered my mind. If I had been Sam, you would have looked up the instant I stepped through that doorway."

Riley shrugged and leaned back in his swivel chair. He grinned, for he was used to this kind of needling from Jim. He said, "I'm an honest man, my friend. I'm also a smart man. I know which side of my bread is buttered. A stupid man don't. Sometimes I think you're pretty damned stupid, Jim. Your pa wasn't. Neither is Rose. Makes a man wonder how it was possible for you to inherit so much stupidity."

Jim nodded. "Does make a man wonder, all right."

He was used to hearing this kind of talk from Buck Riley. They had been friends for years. Riley had grown up on a ranch north of the B-in-a-Box. He was older than Jim, and therefore had always been a little better during their boyhood years with a gun or a rope. He had been a better hunter and fisherman, and a good deal better at breaking horses. So Jim, being younger, had looked up to and respected Riley because he had been able to do so many things well.

The time came when Jim caught up with Riley and could do anything as well as the older man. Still, the friendship had remained on the same firm ground until Riley ran for sheriff and was elected. At that time it seemed to Jim that all the guts Buck Riley ever had simply ran out of him.

On the surface, they were as good friends as ever. They hoorawed each other as they had just done, but now, after the beating Jim had just taken this morning, he didn't feel about Riley as he always had. Was Buck Riley just another straw man that Sam Clegg manipulated any way he wanted to?

For a moment Jim studied Riley's lean, leathery face. He realized that the sheriff had grown up on a ten-cow spread just about the size of the B-in-a-Box, but where Rose and Jim had been Hank Baron's only children, a dozen kids had somehow managed to grow up and find enough to eat on the Riley spread. Now Buck was married and lived in town, and had three little Rileys of his own. As sheriff, he didn't make a big salary, but it was the most he's ever had, and he wasn't in any mood to throw it away.

Now Jim knew he was going to say something that would make Riley sore and he hated to do it. Finally he said, "Buck, I've come to the end of my string. I can't josh about it any more. Maybe I'm as stupid as you say I am, and maybe you're smart the same as almost everybody else in this county is, but by God, when are you gonna get up off your knees?"

The question did sting Riley. He didn't say a word for several seconds, but his face flushed. They'd said this same thing back and forth to each other; it wasn't the words that were said but it was the tone Jim used. The undercurrent had been there before. Now it was out in the open. The effect would have been the same if Jim had leaned across the desk and slapped Riley on the side of the face.

"Get out of here." Riley motioned toward the door. "Get out before I lose my temper."

"No," Jim said. "Go ahead and lose it if you want to, but you'll find it again mighty damned quick. I may kill Dutch Manders and Chick Lund when I feel a little better. They got a gun on me this morning and, along with Bones Porter, beat and kicked hell out of me. Are you going to do anything about it?"

"You know I'm not," Riley snapped. "I can't arrest every cowboy who beats up another one. I'd have this jail crammed all the time if I did."

"It don't make no difference to you that Manders held a gun on me so I couldn't defend myself?"

Riley stared at his desk top. He said sullenly, "No."

"Then you won't do anything to me when I kill those two skunks?"

"Not if it's a fair fight. If you shoot 'em in the back, or if they ain't armed, I'd have to do something."

"All right, Buck." Jim leaned forward and tossed his cigarette stub into the spittoon at the end of the desk. "Let me ask you one question. You're going to have to answer this one sooner or later, so you'd better begin thinking about it. What would Sam and the Cattlemen's Association have to do for you to arrest any of 'em?"

Riley got up and walked to the window and looked out at the weed-covered yard. He jammed his hands into his pockets, holding his shoulders stiff. "I won't answer your question, Jim. Sam won't do anything that I have to arrest him for."

"No, I suppose not. You can always overlook what he does the same as you're overlooking the fact that three men beat me up without giving me a chance to defend myself. Now I'm telling you that you will have one hell of a time overlooking the fact that Sam and his yes-men are hiring a Tom Horn type of assassin if the settlers ain't off the Slow Water in whatever time Sam gave 'em. Can you overlook murder, Buck?"

Riley wheeled to face him. "Come off it, Jim. Where'd you hear a wild yarn like that?"

"Never mind where I heard it. It's what's going to happen. Sam stopped at my place this morning to see where I stood. He said he was warning the farmers today. I also have heard I'm on his list and I'll be murdered if I don't leave the country. I ain't going, Buck. If I turn up with a slug in my back, you'll know where I got it."

Riley's hands were still jammed into his pockets. He glowered at Jim as if not certain whether to believe him or not. Finally he asked, "Where do you stand?"

"I'm a cowman," Jim said. "I sure as hell ain't a farmer, but on the other hand, I've got some purty strong notions about law and order and justice, and we don't have it in this county. I'll never get on my knees the way Pa done and the way Rose wants me to do now, and I told Sam I wouldn't have any part of a trumped-up charge against the farmers for rustling. I don't believe they've done any rustling, but if they have, it's your job to do something about it."

Some of the resentment left Riley. He was listening and thinking, and suddenly he nodded. "It is my job, and I've been up and down the Slow Water looking for evidence of what Sam says has been happening. I don't know whether the grangers have done any rustling or not. All I know is that I didn't find any evidence that they have."

"Well then, if some of 'em turn up murdered . . ."

Riley seemed to catch up with himself then and interrupted angrily, "Just because one of the settlers gets murdered is no proof Sam or the Cattlemen's Association done it. And if I did arrest one of 'em, do you think I'd get a conviction in this county?"

"Oh hell, if there was proof, you'd look the other way, I suppose." Jim got up, the front legs of his chair banging on the floor. "You know what's coming. If you're comfortable staying on your knees, go ahead."

He stalked out of the sheriff's office, so angry he forgot for the moment how much his side hurt. He cooled off when he reached the yard in front of the courthouse. He slowed up, telling himself he had known that was the way it would go with Riley. On one thing Riley was right. He'd never convict Sam Clegg or any member of the Association of any crime in this county. Only the farmers would vote guilty, and they'd never in the world get on a jury.

The Skull horses were still tied in front of the Palace. Jim went on, no longer tempted to go in after Dutch Manders. The job would wait. Manders had too good a thing with Skull to leave the country. He'd be on hand when Jim wanted him.

He reached his buckskin, untied, and mounted. He rode home slowly, his side still hurting. As he rode, he thought about the meeting of the Cattlemen's Association that night and decided not to go. He wouldn't do any more good talking to Sam Clegg and the others than he had talking to Buck Riley.

5

Jim reached the B-in-a-Box late in the afternoon to find Ed Majors hunkered by the corral gate, his pipe in his mouth. It was typical of Rose not to invite Ed to wait in the house. She didn't approve of him and she didn't approve of Jim riding into town with Ed on Saturday nights and spending money on whiskey that had better be spent on buying a good bull or more land or more hay or anything else that would last. Whiskey didn't.

"Howdy, Ed," Jim said as he eased to the ground.

Ed started to say howdy, then saw how carefully Jim was moving and the bruises of his face. He asked, "Has it started?"

"It's started," Jim said, and told him what had happened.

"I'll take care of your horse for you." Ed took the reins, then turned back to Jim. "We've knowed it was coming for a long time. Sam ain't a man to sit on his butt forever when things are going on he don't like. He don't like homesteaders, and he don't like to have a poor man courting his daughter."

Jim eased to the ground and leaned against a corral post as Ed led the buckskin to the log trough. He rolled and lighted a cigarette and smoked until Ed turned the buckskin into the corral and sat down beside him.

Both men were twenty-three, but there the resemblance ended. Ed Majors was a farmer who had settled on the Slow Water more than a year ago. He'd come from Nebraska and said he had a girl back there he figured he'd send for as soon as his farm would support a family, and that, Jim knew, would be a long time.

He was short and stocky with a red face that never tanned. He was as strong as a young bull, he could work in the field all day and want to go out that night and cut his wolf loose. Jim hired him during haying and told Rose he had never seen a better hand, but that didn't impress Rose who said she didn't see what Jim saw in Ed. Jim couldn't tell her. He didn't know, but they got along fine and were the best of neighbors. That was enough for Jim.

Ed filled his pipe and tamped the tobacco down, then fished a match out of a vest pocket as he eyed Jim. "You know why I'm here?"

"I can make a good guess," Jim answered. "Sam Clegg paid you a visit today."

Ed nodded. "Me and the other farmers on the Slow Water. He's given us one week to sell and get out of the country. He'll buy us out at his figure, he told us, if we can't get a better deal. The thing is none of us except Jeremy White have anything much to sell. We're trying to prove up on our place. White pre-empted his, so he's got title to his land and he can sell it. He won't, though."

"Did Sam say what he'd do if you were still here?"

Ed struck a match and held the flame to the tobacco. He puffed on it and blew out the match, then he said, "Not in so many words, but he made it plain enough. He'll burn us out and shoot anybody who fights back."

Jim shook his head. "No. That would be an open and shut case. I mean, you or any of the others who got burned out would recognize him or his men. You could go to Buck Riley and swear out a warrant for Sam's arrest."

"Riley wouldn't do anything," Ed grumbled.

"He'd have to under those conditions," Jim said. "I figure Sam will be a little more sly about it, like sending for a Tom Horn kind of killer and having two or three of you murdered while he was spending the day in town where everybody could see him and know what he was doing."

Ed took the pipe out of his mouth and stared at Jim so long his pipe went cold. "Jim, you don't really believe that?"

Jim nodded. "I do. I'm guessing it will be an operation voted by the Cattlemen's Association on the grounds that if Buck Riley can't or won't stop the rustling, they have to do what they can."

"How'd you hear about it?"

Jim flipped his cigarette stub away and shook his head. "I can't tell you that, but I'm sure it's straight. Sam notified me there was a meeting of the Cattlemen's Association at his place tonight. I've got a vote, but I'm not sure I feel like riding to Skull."

"You'd be smart not to," Ed said. "They'll kill you if you buck 'em."

"They'd better kill me," Jim said. "If they don't, I'm going to play hell with 'em. I've been thinking about going to Cheyenne to see the governor. I don't suppose he'll do anything. He was a friend of Pa's and Sam's years ago, so he'll probably say Sam wouldn't do a thing like that, but I'd like to have it on the record."

Ed lighted his pipe again. He said, "We're gonna fight. Jeremy White's called a meeting for tonight, but none of us figured on anything like that. No man can protect himself against a drygulcher if they can find one."

"They'll find him," Jim said. "Some were operating when Tom Horn was, and even after Horn was arrested. They're still in the country. The funny part of it is that a man like Sam and the other members of the Association can convince themselves that it's a decent and honorable way to settle the trouble."

"You know Jeremy White?" Ed asked. "Really know him?"

Jim shook his head. "Does anybody?"

"Not really, I guess," Ed said. "He never talks about where he came from or what he did before he settled on the Slow Water. We all neighbor some and we've got a little church we go to, and we have picnics and parties in the winter, so we visit and gab and have a good time, but Jeremy, he always comes and wants to be a part of everything, only he acts like he never lived a day before he got here. I mean, he don't mention what his life was like before he came to this country."

"Doc Ashton mentioned him today," Jim said thoughtfully. "He seems to think that White is just as mean and crazy as Sam."

Ed shook his head. "I don't think so, but he's a fighter. He talked up to Sam one day in the Palace, you know. He don't usually wear a gun, but he was wearing it that day. He's the only farmer who's got enough money to hire a couple of men and they were with him. Sam was alone and he backed down."

"Where'd he get his money?"

"None of us know, but we'd sure like to," Ed answered. "I tell you he never opens his mouth. Even his wife and boy don't say anything about his past, and usually kids talk to other kids."

"The boy and his mother are in Cheyenne, ain't they?" Jim asked.

"Yeah, the boy's been sick and Ashton ain't been able to help him, so he sent them to a specialist in Cheyenne." Ed scratched the back of his neck, frowning. "I wonder why Doc thought he was mean and crazy like Clegg?"

"He didn't say. He just said that White would get you to stand and fight."

Ed rose. "Well, I gotta get home and milk so I can get to the meeting." He scratched the back of his neck again, his gaze on Jim. Finally he said, "Son, we're in the same boat. Sam's after all of us. He wants our land and he's hounding you to keep you from marrying Carrie. We both may be dead in four or five days."

"The odds are pretty good that it'll go that way," Jim agreed. "You're saying we'd better slope out of here so we can go on living?"

"Hell no," Ed said, "but I was thinking that maybe you ought to come to White's meeting tonight. You ain't no farmer, but we're on the same side just the same."

"Think they'll let me in?"

"I'll get you in."

"I'll see how I feel after supper," Jim said.

Ed mounted. "Make it if you can," he said, and rode away.

Jim pulled himself to his feet. He stood motionless for

a moment, watching Ed until he disappeared downstream, then he walked to the house.

Rose was putting supper on the table. She said tartly, "I was just waiting for your friend to go home. I've had supper ready for an hour."

Jim pumped a pan of water. He washed and dried, then ran a comb through his heavy black hair. "I guess you didn't think of inviting him in for supper."

"No, I certainly did not," she snapped. "You going to the meeting at Skull?"

"No," he said as he sat down.

Rose frowned. "Maybe you could get your bridges rebuilt if you did."

Jim didn't say anything. He filled his plate and started to eat. Rebuilding his bridges was the last thing he planned to do. He glanced up at Rose once. She had a waspish temper, but she didn't let go at him as she often did. She was eating, her mind on something a long ways from here, he thought. She must have noticed the way he walked and the bruises on his face, but she hadn't asked what had happened.

He saw the deep lines of discontent around her green eyes; he mentally measured her long nose and sharp chin, and he lowered his gaze to his plate. He was ashamed of himself, but he couldn't help thinking that she looked exactly like the pictures of witches he used to look at in the books of fairy stories he read when he was a boy.

When he finished eating, he went outside. He sat on the porch and smoked and watched the day die. He wasn't going anywhere tonight. He hurt so much he didn't feel like doing anything except go to bed, and then he probably wouldn't sleep.

6

When Sam Clegg returned from delivering his warnings to the settlers on the Slow Water, he sent his three men back to Skull and rode to the B-in-a-Box alone. He hoped he wouldn't see Jim Baron.

He wasn't afraid of Jim. He wasn't afraid of any man. Not even that tough little bastard, Jeremy White, who had looked him straight in the eyes that time in the Palace and said, "Go to hell." It was just that he wanted to talk to Rose and he could do more with her if she was alone than if Jim was there.

He reined up in front of the house and stepped down. The buckskin wasn't in the corral, so Jim was probably gone. As Clegg turned toward the front door, Rose came out and held the screen open.

"Come in, Mr. Clegg," she said.

"I don't have time to come in, Rose," he said. "Is Jim home?"

"No." Rose frowned. "I don't know where he is. He rode off this morning just after you were here. He . . . he wouldn't tell me anything. He just said he'd be home for supper."

"Good," Clegg said. "You're the one I wanted to see anyway and I'm glad you're alone. You see, we may have a little trouble shaping up on this range, and I don't want you and Jim to be involved. Your pa and me were good friends. I'm anxious to continue that friendship with you and Jim."

"I'm anxious, too," she said worriedly. "More anxious than you know. As far as I'm concerned, I'll do anything you want us to, but Jim's making me a lot of trouble. He never gave his father any trouble as long as he was alive, but now he says he's running the outfit and I can run the house. I just can't manage him, Mr. Clegg."

"You'll have to," Clegg said harshly. "I guess all of us have lost stock in the last year except you and Jim. We've gone as far as we can with these thieving nesters that have moved in on us. I'm just coming back from warning them to leave the country. I'm hoping Jim won't throw in with them."

"He won't." Rose's thin lips squeezed together, her sharp chin held high. "I'll see that he don't."

"Then I'll count on that," Clegg said, and turned away.

"Mr. Clegg," Rose called.

He turned back. He said impatiently, "Yes?"

"I'm worried about something else," Rose said. "If Jim and Carrie get married . . ."

"They won't," Clegg interrupted. "I promise you they won't. I have other plans for Carrie."

Rose's smile was as wintry as the expression in her green eyes. "Thank you, Mr. Clegg. I guess I'm selfish, but I do want to protect my home. You know what they say about two women under one roof."

"I know, and it's true," Clegg said. "All I can tell you is that if Jim brings another woman under your roof, it will not be my daughter."

He turned and strode to his horse. Mounting, he glanced again at the corral. The buckskin still wasn't there. He rode toward the ridge to the south, and when he reached the top, he paused a moment to blow his horse.

Looking downstream, he saw a rider coming toward the B-in-a-Box. The man was a long ways off, but from the sloppy way he rode, Clegg decided he was one of the settlers, probably Ed Majors coming to see Jim.

Sam Clegg turned his horse toward Skull, thinking about Majors. He was just another red-faced farmer, no different from his neighbors except that he was younger and he was single. The only man among the settlers who was different was that damned flinty-eyed Jeremy White. He'd be the first they'd rub out. After that the others would scatter. All but Ed Majors.

Majors was a problem because he and Jim Baron were

friends. Clegg simply could not understand Jim. Somehow he'd managed to be born with a ramrod down his back that wouldn't bend. Clegg didn't know where he'd got it. His father hadn't had it and his mother had been a meek woman. Rose wasn't meek, but she wasn't stupid enough to fight for no reason.

Clegg didn't think his visit had done any good, although he knew it was something he'd had to do just on the slim chance it might work. Rose couldn't manage Jim. That was where the rub came. Majors might be able to drag Jim into the fight on the side of the grangers. Clegg didn't want that to happen. If Jim and Jeremy White were on the same side, the fight might be tough, and there was no reason for that to happen if everything was managed right.

If Ed Majors was killed when the fracas started . . . Well, it was worth thinking about. The trouble was you couldn't be sure which way it would work. Majors' death might stampede the whole bunch right off the Slow Water, leaving White to make his fight alone. On the other hand, it might throw Jim in with them. Clegg decided he'd have to think it over.

The sun was almost down when he rode into Skull's yard, the horizon to the west on both sides of Laramie Peak turning scarlet. He always enjoyed riding in this way and seeing the buildings spread out before him. He had built well and carefully, looking to the future, and he was inordinately proud of what he had done.

The house was a log structure with a huge, stone fireplace on the west end. He had picked this building site years ago among a dozen or more scattered pines, with a small tributary of the South Fork running past the house. Water was piped into both the house and the bunkhouse, and another pipe fed the big trough by the corral.

The layout had been carefully planned, with practical efficiency foremost in his mind, the way a man would build. The barns and corrals were solid. No flowers. A vegetable garden above the buildings along the creek so it could be irrigated. A chicken shed. A pigpen downstream so it wouldn't pollute the water and be far enough away so the stench seldom reached the house.

Most ranchers never bothered with these things, but Sam Clegg hired two men who did nothing but take care of the garden, the chickens, and the pigs, and do the butchering and smoking of the meat. It had paid off, and he knew he had a smaller bill at the Mercantile in Wheat-ridge than any other big rancher in the valley because the bulk of the food was raised right here within half a mile of his house.

He took a long breath, pride rolling through him as it did every time he saw his ranch when he'd been away, even for a few hours, pride because he had started the same as Hank Baron and the rest, but he had done much more. He had been a better planner than the others, a harder driver, and more ruthless.

Sam Clegg liked the word ruthless. It had the same flavor in his mind as success. Indeed, it was the major cause of his success. It was the reason people looked up to him and respected him, it was the reason the other members of the Association would do exactly as he told them. It was the reason that within a week, or at the most two weeks, the settlers would be off the Slow Water.

Not that he had to have the land where the farmers had settled. It was a proposition that the time had come to take it. Life was geared to one basic law. To live was to keep growing, to die was to stop growing. It was as simple as that.

Charley Pipp, the gangly chore boy, came out of the barn and took his horse. Clegg turned toward the house as Bones Porter left the bunkhouse and strode across the yard, calling, "Boss, I want to talk to you."

Clegg waited impatiently. He was anxious to go in and wash up and give Carrie a nudge if supper wasn't ready. The other members of the Cattlemen's Association would be here soon and he wanted to be ready for them.

When Porter reached him, he said, "We followed Miss Carrie like you told us to. She met Jim Baron over on the North Fork. They talked a while, then she left. We waited till she was gone. He stayed on the creek, acting like he was thinking things out real careful. We didn't have no trouble getting the drop on him. I guess he was worrying about Miss Carrie."

Porter stopped and cleared his throat. Clegg asked, "Is he still alive?"

"Yeah, he's alive, but he's bunged up some." Porter cleared his throat. "God damn it, Boss. I ain't one bit proud of myself. It don't take much guts to beat and kick a man when he's got a gun on him and he can't make a fight out of it."

"He's been told to stay away from Carrie," Clegg said. "Maybe now he'll get out of the country. I hope he does. Then we won't have to kill him."

"I figure you've got the wrong man," Porter said. "He's a tough one. He ain't gonna run."

"Then he's the one who makes the decision about living or dying," Clegg said, and walked on to the house, leaving Porter scowling at his back.

He hung his hat on the antler rack by the door, stripped off his gun belt, and hung it up, then crossed the room to the kitchen. Porter was too soft to work for Skull, he told himself. Dutch Manders and Chick Lund were more to his liking. Maybe he ought to fire Porter. You didn't build an outfit like Skull by being soft.

Carrie was frying meat at the stove. Clegg walked to the sink, ran water into the tin basin, and washed and combed his hair. For a moment he stared at himself in the mirror above the sink. He liked what he saw. A few lines in his face and around his eyes, but they came from squinting at the sun and not from age. He didn't have a gray hair in his head.

He'd thought about remarrying. Now that Carrie was grown and would soon be gone, he'd better start looking around. Nora Bain, Carrie's best friend and the daughter of the storekeeper, Larry Bain, was young and pretty and a good housekeeper. It was time he started courting her.

"How soon will supper be ready?" he asked.

"In about ten minutes," Carrie answered.

He nodded and walked out of the kitchen, knowing she had not heard about the beating Jim Baron had taken or she would have got on his back about it. He crossed the long living room to his office at one end and sat down at the desk. He tipped his swivel chair back and looked up at the framed picture of Napoleon on the wall.

By God, there was a man.

7

When Ed Majors reached Jeremy White's place at dusk, he was surprised to find every other settler on the Slow Water there ahead of him. They had gathered in front of the house. White had hung a lantern on a post and stood beside it, a sheet of paper in his hands. His two hired men were behind him.

Ed stepped down, tied at the hitch rail, and approached the settlers, counting them again as he had when he first rode up. Eight men, nine now that he had joined them. With White and his two, there was a total of twelve. If they were all willing to fight, twelve were enough to make trouble for Sam Clegg and the Cattlemen's Association.

"We're glad to see you, Ed," White said. "You're the one we've been waiting for. Parson, this calls for a prayer. Then we'll get down to the dirty business that faces us."

Parson Bean lived next to Ed, a tall, raw-boned man with a white beard, a skinny wife, and eight children. He wasn't really a preacher, but he was the best they had. The settlers and their wives and children held church service every Sunday morning in the schoolhouse. Bean didn't do much except read the Bible and pray and exhort the people to praise God and fight the devil, but the church was a factor in holding the little community of farmers together and Ed knew that was important.

Bean raised both arms and looked up at the darkening sky and bellowed in a great voice as if he were convinced God was deaf. "Our Father who art in Heaven, we ask you to confound our enemies and heap destruction upon them just as the Philistines were once confounded and destroyed by Thy chosen people. Amen."

Several other men added their "Amens," then were silent as White's gaze moved from one settler to another. Ed wondered if White was trying to weigh their courage.

No one could guess how much fight would be in a group of men who dug their living out of the soil, but Ed never doubted the fight that was in Jeremy White. Probably in his hired men, too, or he wouldn't have them on the place.

This was one of the few times Ed had seen White carry a gun, and although it looked as big as a cannon because White was a small man not over five feet two inches, it seemed as natural on him as the tight, little black mustache he wore. Again Ed wondered what the man's background was. The thought occurred to him that White might have been a professional gunfighter, although the idea of a gunfighter turning farmer was ridiculous.

"Gentlemen," White said, "we were all visited by Sam Clegg and three of his tough hands. It seems incredible that in this day and age, and in an organized county with a duly elected sheriff, a thing like this could happen, but the fact is it did. Clegg accused us of rustling his cattle. I will admit to you, although I didn't to him, that the White family has eaten Skull beef. I would guess that the Skull punchers have eaten B-in-a-Box beef or maybe Alred's Rafter A beef. In any case, we haven't rustled him blind as he accused us of doing.

"Clegg made himself clear to me. I think he did to all of you. We sell out to him for a fraction of what our land is worth, or he'll raid up and down this valley and burn us out and kill us if we resist. We have one week to decide. Gentlemen, it is my opinion we have decided. We will not sell. We will resist, and by God, before we're done, we'll make Sam Clegg sorry he ever had this idea."

Parson Bean said, "Amen." Others nodded. Ed, glancing at the men around him in the murky light of the lantern, was surprised. They would fight. He looked at White, at his thin, sun-blackened face, his strong chin, his tough little body with the revolver on his hip, and then Ed's gaze returned to White's face. His eyes were hot and bright, the eyes of a killer, and suddenly Ed remembered Jim saying that Doc Ashton had claimed Jeremy

White was as tough and mean as Clegg. If anyone could confound the Lord's enemies, it was Jeremy White.

"All right," White went on, "we've had plenty of time to think about this. Patrick Henry said to give him liberty or death. That same principle has been fought for time after time in the history of man. It's just as important to us here in Wyoming on the banks of the Slow Water as it was in Patrick Henry's time. None of us wants to die, but maybe some of us will. If there is a man here who wants out, get on your horse and ride out and be off the river by morning."

No one moved. A chill raced down Ed's spine. They were all trapped. None of them had any choice. If you ran, Jeremy White would have your hide, and if you didn't, Sam Clegg would have it.

A moment later the chill was gone. Ed Majors knew only one thing for sure about this mess. If he was going to get rubbed out in the next few days or weeks, he'd rather do it fighting Sam Clegg than Jeremy White.

White held up the paper that was in his right hand. "Gentlemen, we must have some kind of an organization. We've got to understand that once we start down this road, we cannot turn back. If you sign this paper, and then want out, I'll shoot you myself, I won't wait for one of Clegg's killers to do it. Therefore it seems to me we have to take an oath. This is what I have: 'I, the undersigned, before God swear that I will defend my farm against attack with my life. I will take Jeremy White's orders in making this defense.'"

White looked up from the paper. "Believe me, I am not looking for more trouble or power or anything else, but somebody has to lead. If you choose to scratch my name out and put down Pastor Bean or any other name, I will sign it right along with the rest of you."

"No, no." Bean stepped up and reached for the paper and pencil in White's hand. "You're the man."

They signed one by one. Ed was the last, and when he gave the paper and pencil back to White, he said, "Jerry, I was talking to Jim Baron just a little while ago. He says

Clegg will not raid and burn us out, but the Cattlemen's Association is hiring a Tom Horn type of killer who will drygulch us one after another until the rest of us panic and run."

White's mouth curled in contempt. "Where did he hear that yarn?"

"He didn't say."

"Forget it. He's a cowman. He belongs to the Association. He's no different than Sam Clegg or Ace Alred or any of the others. He was just trying to scare you."

"No he wasn't," Ed said more sharply than he intended. "I asked him to come tonight to the meeting, but he was beaten up by three Skull punchers this morning. I guess he didn't feel like making the ride."

"It's a good thing he didn't come because I would have sent him home," White said harshly. "He would have been here to spy for the Association, and we can't afford to risk that. Now my first order is for every one of you to be here by seven o'clock Saturday night. We won't wait for Clegg. We'll show him what he's up against, and it might be enough to make him back down. Bring a white sack or a pillow case. Cut eye holes. When we ride into Wheatridge we'll be White Caps. I'll write out a warning and we'll nail it up on the courthouse door. Bring your Winchesters. We'll carry them across our saddles in plain view.

"Just one more thing. In the morning my men and myself will build a pile of brush on top of the bluff north of the river. If anything happens that means we've got to fight, we'll fire the brush. All of you can see it from your houses. Saddle up, bring your rifles, and get here as fast as you can. If you don't have plenty of ammunition, get to town and stock up."

Ed was the first to mount and ride home. He was sore at White for dismissing so lightly the information Jim had given him. It had been even worse for him to say he would have sent Jim home as a spy. Still, White didn't know Jim except by sight, and this was a natural assumption for him to make. The ugly truth was that Jim stood alone. The settlers wouldn't have him and Clegg was determined to run him out of the country or kill him.

When Ed reached his place, he was jumpy at the thought that in a few days a killer might be hiding in the willows along the river ready to shoot him. He stripped gear from his horse and turned him into the corral.

He walked across the yard to his house, and sat down on the step and filled his pipe and lit it. The house wasn't really a house at all, but a tarpaper shack that wasn't fit for a woman to live in if he sent for his girl. The barn wasn't really a barn, either. It was just a slab shed that didn't give his cow or team or saddle horse much protection against cold weather, and Wyoming winters were cold.

He put his pipe down on the ground and wrapped his arms around his knees and rocked back and forth. He didn't have anything. Not a damn thing, and right now he had little hope that he would ever have anything if he stayed on this homestead.

At that moment Ed Majors felt as if he were a little boy who wanted to cry and couldn't. If he had a lick of sense, he'd sell to Clegg for anything he could get and ride out of here before he was murdered, but he knew he couldn't do it.

8

Rose Baron was furious. She was trapped. She had reached the point where she felt she couldn't go on living in the same house with Jim. Yet she needed him. He was bullheaded and insensitive, he thought he knew it all, and he wouldn't listen to a thing she said. He acted as if he owned all the ranch and not just half of it.

The part she could not understand was that he had seemed willing to work for their father and take his orders, but the moment Hank Baron died, Jim changed. He actually acted as if he wanted to fight Sam Clegg. That was stupid any way you looked at it.

What was the sense of fighting a man when you didn't have the slightest chance of winning? The other ranchers in the county knew that and they swallowed their pride if that was what it took and followed Sam Clegg's lead. Why couldn't Jim be as smart as the rest of them were? Of course he was in love with Carrie. He'd get over that, but she wasn't so sure he would get over being contrary with Sam Clegg.

She was trapped because she had come to the place where she hated Jim, but she could not get along without him. The ranch wasn't big enough to afford a hired hand. Even if it was, she couldn't bring one here to live with her in this house. Everybody would be horrified. Besides, it would be dangerous.

She rattled and banged the dishes as she washed and dried them and put them away. Their father had always listened to her. She knew it had gone against his grain to kow-tow to Sam Clegg, but she used to tell him they had to have a living, and as long as they were Clegg's friend, they'd get along. They worked roundup together, they drove to the railroad together, and if Hank Baron ever needed someone to co-sign a note at the bank, Clegg did it. The arrangement was a good one because it gave the Barons as much security as it was possible to have. If her father became rebellious as he did sometimes about doing everything Clegg asked, Rose always told him he couldn't risk losing that security.

She would say that security was important to a woman, that she was willing to stay home and take care of him and Jim, but if he was going to just throw away everything they had spent years building, why, she'd go to town and get a job and he could just hire a housekeeper.

She had no intentions of doing any such thing, but the threat was enough to curb her father's rebellion. He had leaned on her more and more after her mother's death. She had encouraged that. The trouble with Jim was he didn't lean on her or anyone else.

As she put the last dish away in the cupboard, she looked around at her neat kitchen. It was spotless. She took great pride in that. Her father used to tell her she was the best housekeeper in Slow Water County, a compliment that always pleased her, but Jim never said anything of the kind. A spotless house didn't mean a thing to him.

Every day it seemed Jim would come in with horse manure on his boots from the corral and she'd have to scrub the floor for an hour. She'd raise Cain about it, but it never seemed to make any difference. He was careless, even indifferent to the things she wanted.

Now, standing here in the room which had been hers and hers alone for twenty years, the thought of losing it because of Jim's stupid pride was more than she could bear. Suddenly she began to cry.

She hadn't cried for years. She considered it a weakness and she had no use for weakness. Quickly she went into her bedroom because she didn't want Jim to hear her and shut the door. She lay down. She put a hand over her mouth; she wiped her eyes with a handkerchief she held in the other hand.

She tried to stop, but she couldn't. It was too much. She just couldn't stay here with Jim treating her this way, but she had no place to go. She had no money. The thought of going to Wheatridge or Cheyenne and keeping house for someone was intolerable.

Then, out of nowhere, the startling thought came to her that she owned half of B-in-a-Box and there might be some legal way of handling Jim, of making him do what she wanted him to do so he couldn't risk her half of the ranch as well as his simply because he was too stiff-necked to recognize reality. The thing to do was to go into town and see Judge Carr who had always done whatever legal work her father had required.

Once the idea occurred to her, she could not wait until morning. She got up and left the bedroom and crossed the kitchen and the front room, her heels pounding on the floor in grim determination. She let the screen close with a bang and went past Jim without saying a word.

She was off the porch and halfway across the yard when Jim asked, "Where are you going?"

She didn't turn, she didn't say a word, she kept right on to the barn. He hadn't told her anything this morning about where he was going. She still didn't know where he went. She wasn't going to tell him anything now. She harnessed her driving mare and hooked her to the buggy and got in.

Jim was on his feet when she drove toward him. He tried to stop her, but he didn't move very fast. She'd noticed at supper that he was hurt. She'd seen the bruises on his face, too, but he hadn't offered an explanation and she wasn't going to lower herself by asking. He'd been in a fight, she guessed, and had got the worst of it.

She sailed past him, her head held high, her chin thrust forward. Let him worry about her for a change. It would be good for him.

She reached Wheatridge with twilight almost gone. She stopped in front of Judge Carr's home, tied the lines around the whipstock, and walked to the house and rang the bell. The judge opened the door a moment later, peered at her in the near darkness, and asked, "Why, Rose, what brings you to town this time of evening?"

"I've got to see you, Judge," she said. "I've got to have some advice."

She realized she sounded almost hysterical and that annoyed her because she hated hysterical women above everything else. She saw that the judge was astonished, and perhaps annoyed, too.

He hesitated, staring at her questioningly, then he said, "Come in," and led the way into the parlor.

He lighted a lamp on the walnut center table and replaced the chimney, the long colored glass drops that hung from the bottom of the shade swaying for a moment. He motioned for her to sit down on the black, leather sofa, then took a cigar out of his pocket as he dropped into a rocking chair.

"You're having trouble with Jim, aren't you?" he asked.

"How did you know?" she demanded.

He shrugged. "It was bound to come. I warned Hank about it when I drew up his will. I told him he should fix it so one of you would have to sell out to the other, but he wouldn't do it."

Rose stared at him for a long moment, then she asked stiffly, "I still don't understand how you knew we wouldn't get along."

"You're two willful people," he said. "It's pretty simple when you think about it. I'm surprised Hank couldn't see what would happen. For instance, if Jim got married and brought his wife into your house, you'd have nothing but trouble. Is that what's going to happen?"

"No." She didn't like being called willful. The word applied to Jim, not to her. "I've given my life to keeping house for my father and then Jim. Half of the ranch is mine, therefore I have a right to help make decisions that affect the future of the ranch."

"Would you help make the decisions?" he asked. "Or would you make them and expect Jim to carry them out?"

She flushed, anger growing in her. "I'd help make them."

Judge Carr leaned back and chewed on his cigar. "What is the advice you want?"

She poured out her story, how that Sam Clegg had always been the leader of the cowmen, that her father had been willing to go along with Clegg, and Judge Carr knew as well as anyone that Clegg got what he wanted in Slow Water County.

When she said that, Carr took the cigar out of his mouth, his white mustache bristling. "Rose, that's a hard thing to say. Most of us living in town hesitate to say it so bluntly, but from a practical point of view, you're right."

"Of course I'm right," she cried. "We have to accept it, but Jim won't. When Sam came by this morning, Jim ran into the house and strapped his gun belt on. Why, he just as much as defied Sam by doing that."

"More power to him," the judge said grimly. "I wish I had that much courage. Or Buck Riley or any of the rest of us in town."

"No, Judge, no," Rose protested. "That's not the way to get along with Sam. I've got to know how I can make Jim do what I want him to. I won't let him destroy my half of the ranch as well as his own share by fighting Sam. I don't know what's going to happen, but Sam stopped late this afternoon and warned me about Jim getting mixed up in whatever trouble is coming with the nesters. I . . . I can't handle Jim, but I told Sam I could keep Jim from throwing in with the nesters. Now I know I can't. If he does, we'll be destroyed."

"Rose, there is no way you can make Jim do what you want him to." Judge Carr got up. "I'm sorry, but I have a meeting I've got to attend."

She struggled to her feet, her hands clenched. This was not what she had expected to hear and certainly not what she wanted to hear. "Judge, there must be a way I can keep him from . . ."

"Buy him out, Rose. Or sell to him."

He walked out of the room and along the hall to the front door. She followed him, walking stiffly, so angry she could not risk saying a word. Judge Carr was on Jim's side and that was crazy.

"Good night, Rose," the judge said.

She left the house without saying a word and walked to her buggy. She got in and drove away. The darkness was complete now except for the starlight. She put her mare away when she got home and went into the house.

Jim was in bed. As soon as he heard her come in, he called, "Where have you been?"

She stopped in the doorway of his bedroom. She said in the tight voice she used when she was furious, a tone Jim had heard many times. "Someway I'm going to keep you from letting Sam Clegg destroy us. I don't know how, but I will."

She went on into her bedroom and lay down with her clothes on. She stared into the darkness, thinking about Jim, about Clegg and what lay ahead, but she did not find any answers to her questions. All she could see was disaster. The thought that Clegg might lose to the settlers never occurred to her.

9

Sam Clegg stood in the front of the Skull ranch house as the members of the Cattlemen's Association rode in. He shook hands with each man as he dismounted and asked about his children and his wife and how he was getting along. This was his way. Actually he cared nothing about the answers to his questions, but he was so skillful pretending to be interested that no one suspected the truth.

When all of them had arrived, he said, "Let's go in, gentlemen." He led the way into the house and shut the front door. He passed a box of Havana cigars around the small circle, poured a drink of excellent whiskey for each, then shut the door that opened into the kitchen.

He sat down and nodded at Vance Malone, the secretary. "The meeting will come to order. Vance, read the minutes of the previous meeting."

Malone read them. They were innocuous enough, for Clegg had laid the foundation of tonight's meeting by private conversations with each man here. The only member of the Association he had not talked to about it was Jim Baron, and he was satisfied that Jim would not show up tonight.

When Malone finished, Clegg asked, "Are there any corrections or alterations? If not, the minutes will stand approved as read. Is there any old business?"

No one said a word, although Nick Dillon who owned Wineglass just south of Skull looked at Clegg sharply, then lowered his eyes to the floor. Dillon had been the least enthusiastic of any of them to Clegg's plan, and now the disturbing thought struck Clegg that maybe Jim Baron had undermined him and had talked to Dillon. He dismissed the idea at once for the simple reason that Jim and Dillon were not good friends, and Jim would have no way of knowing how Dillon felt.

"All right," Clegg said, "we will go on to new business. I've talked to each of you about our losses and about the seriousness of the nester problem that faces us. We know what has happened on other ranges when the settlers began moving in. John Hunton was one of the best of the early cattlemen in eastern Wyoming. At one time he had fenced 14,000 acres. The government made him take his fence down, and you all know how the settlers flocked in like the proverbial locusts."

He cleared his throat, glancing briefly at Dillon who was still staring at the floor. "Gentlemen, our choice is clear. We take strong measures now or we are whipped. The eight or ten families now living on the Slow Water will not destroy us, but they are only the beginning. In the end we will be destroyed if we don't move them out because their presence will encourage others to come. On the other hand, if we moved them out now, new ones will know what they're up against and they won't try it."

Ace Alred nodded. His Rafter A was the second largest spread in the county and he was worried about his future. He said angrily, "We should have got the first one, Sam."

Clegg looked at him. "I know that." He tongued his cigar to the other side of his mouth. "But it wouldn't have worked. Do you know why?"

"I know why, all right." Alred looked around the circle contemptuously. "We've got too many nervous Nellies in this outfit. That's why. The worst one is Jim Baron, but he ain't the only one. We had to wait until enough grangers came in to scare us, but I ain't real sure now that anybody's scared but you and me."

Malone looked up from his secretary's book. "I'm scared, but it ain't because I've lost a lot of cattle. I ain't. It's just that I know what's happened on other ranges. If we wait one more year, we might just as well sell out."

"If we can find a few fools who will buy a dead horse," Alred grumbled.

"Let's get on with the plan," Clegg said. "I'm willing to put up a thousand dollars in cash if the rest of you throw five hundred into the kitty. That will give us thirty-five hundred. It should be enough to do the job." He nodded at Alred. "Ace knows a man who will take the contract. Do you think it's enough?"

"It'll do for a start," Alred said.

He was a tall, bronzed man who had come to Slow Water County shortly after Clegg and Hank Baron had come. He had worked hard and he had prospered, and, like Clegg, he would do anything to hold what he had.

He was the only cowman in the room Clegg fully and completely trusted, and the reason he did was the simple fact that a human life was not as important to Alred as the future of his ranch. He would have said it plain out if it had been necessary just as Clegg would have said it, but they were the only men in the room who would have been as blunt and callous about it.

A pause followed Alred's remark, then Dillon burst out, "What you mean, a start?"

Alred's pale blue eyes turned to Dillon. "You know damned well what I mean. I don't know what it'll take to get these punkin' rollers to move out. If we've got to raise twice that much money to get the job done, then by God, let's raise it."

"We're talking about murder," Dillon shouted. "You ain't said it, but that's what you're talking about. What the hell, Sam? We can't just . . . just go down the same path that other ranchers have gone."

Clegg pinned his gaze on Dillon. He said, "Nick, we've got our tail in a crack. You're no better off than the rest of us. Are you willing to sit on your butt and see everything you've worked for go to hell because we did nothing when we could have?"

"No, but murder . . ."

Clegg made an impatient gesture. "Murder's an ugly word, Nick. It ain't the right word and you know it. I spent the day riding down the Slow Water. I saw personally every settler on the river and I warned him. I made it plain enough. If they're gone in a week like I told 'em, I say fine. If not, then I say we've got to take steps. Or have you got a better idea in your head?"

"No." Dillon sucked in a long breath. "No, I ain't, and that's the sorry part of this whole business."

"Don't use that word murder again," Alred said harshly. "It ain't murder, not after Sam has gone to the trouble of warning 'em. I'm glad Jim Baron ain't here because he's a stubborn fool who would buck us. I want this unanimous. If anything goes sour, we stand together. If we do, none of us will get hurt."

Clegg nodded. "Right." He smiled. "I might add that I know the governor. All of us know Buck Riley and Judge Carr. There will be no trouble."

"What do you want me to write down in the minutes?" Malone asked.

"Make a simple statement that plans were made to protect our interest." Clegg smiled again, this time without the slightest trace of humor. "No details about hiring an exterminator are necessary."

Malone nodded.

"Then it's understood," Alred said, "that as soon as the week is up, I'll go to Cheyenne and contact my man."

"That's correct," Clegg said. "I expect him to be a careful operator. He can work out of Skull as long as he can find a legitimate reason for being here."

"He'll find one," Alred said.

"Then I declare the meeting adjourned," Clegg said.

He passed the cigars again and sent the whiskey bottle around. The men sat and talked for a few minutes about trivial things: politics and having Teddy Roosevelt in the White House now instead of William McKinley and the condition of the range. Clegg shook hands with them again as they left, but he felt a tension he had not felt before. They were sorry they had made an agreement that might end in murder, he thought, but they'd made it and they were stuck with it.

Alred lingered after the others had gone. He said bluntly, "We made a mistake, Sam. You and me should have done this ourselves."

Clegg shook his head. "I don't think so. Jim Baron wasn't here to vote against us, and no one who was here objected to the plan, so it's unanimous. They've got to back us."

"They will if everything works out and they find out we've saved their spreads," Alred grumbled. "I don't trust 'em in a pinch, Sam."

Clegg's smile was humorless. "It's been my experience you can't trust anybody in a pinch." Then he shrugged. "But they'll be afraid to say anything. I'll settle personally with any of 'em who kick up the least little bit of dust."

"Well, unless I hear from you," Alred said, "I'll take the Monday stage to Cheyenne. Or ride. Maybe that would be better."

"Good." Clegg nodded. "I'll keep an eye on the nesters, but I don't expect 'em to move an inch. Not till there's a funeral or two, and then they'll be on their way in a hurry."

Alred mounted. He sat his saddle for a moment, looking down at Clegg, then he said slowly, "Sam, are you sure this is the only way?"

Clegg was surprised. So even Ace Alred had his doubts. Clegg said, "Sure there's another way. We can take our crews and raid 'em. We can burn 'em out and shoot a few of 'em. You know what will happen?"

"I know," Alred said. "Even Buck Riley would have to do something. We wouldn't be convicted, I guess, but it would raise a hell of a stink until the governor might get into the fracas."

"That's right," Clegg agreed. "This way you and me and the rest of 'em can be in town when it happens. Your man ain't gonna talk. You'n me and the other members of the Association ain't gonna talk because we know it'll put a rope on our necks, so how can they prove anything on us?"

Alred nodded. "It listens good," he said. "So long, Sam."

"So long, Ace."

Alred rode away and Clegg went back into the house. He opened the door into the dining room and walked on back to the kitchen. Carrie wasn't there, so she must have gone to bed. He returned to the front room, took a cigar out of the box, and bit off the end. He lighted it and sat down in his favorite chair, a huge, black leather affair that was the most expensive piece of furniture in the house. It was comfortable and he had never regretted paying what he had for it.

He leaned back, savoring the flavor of the cigar, and raised his eyes to the picture of Napoleon. Here was a man who had dreamed big dreams; he had started from nothing and had become the greatest man in the world before he had gone down.

Clegg wondered how many men Napoleon had lost at Marengo, at Austerlitz, at Waterloo. How many of the enemy had been killed? Their deaths had never worried him in the least, and Sam Clegg did not intend to be worried about how many settlers died here in Slow Water County.

He took the cigar out of his mouth and laughed softly. He might not be the greatest man in the world, but he'd certainly be the greatest man in Wyoming, and that, he told himself, would do for a starter.

10

By Saturday night most of the soreness in Jim's side was gone. The bruises on his face were dark and ugly, and shaving had been a delicate and painful operation, but he had completed it. He saddled up and left the ranch as the dusk light was fading, a cool breeze beginning to flow down from the Laramie range to the west.

As he rode away, he saw Rose standing on the porch staring at him. He could feel her anger even at this distance. She had been furious with him ever since she had left the house and driven away that evening. He still didn't know where she had gone or why. All he knew was that she had been filled with tight-lipped rage since then.

Tonight as he had got up from the table after supper, Rose had asked, "Is there some way I can buy you out?"

"No," he had said.

Now he wondered why she had asked a foolish question like that, knowing how much work he had put into the ranch. She knew, too, that she had no money to buy his half and she wasn't stupid enough to think the bank would loan it to her. More than that, she certainly knew the place had to have one man, probably two if they were hired hands, and she couldn't pay them even if she could find men who would come here and work.

She was angry at him because he wouldn't knuckle under to Sam Clegg. She knew as well as he did that trouble was going to pop before long and these few days of quiet were the clam before the storm. Maybe she still hoped he would make peace with Clegg, although she should know him better than that.

He couldn't guess when or how the storm would hit. All he knew was that he hadn't left the country and sooner or later Chick Lund or Dutch Manders or one of the other Skull hard cases would show up to finish what they'd started. Or, and this thought always sent a chill down his spine, one of these mornings he might walk out of the house and run into a bullet fired by a drygulcher hiding out there in the grass.

He rode downstream toward Ed Majors' farm, deciding that Clegg would not send the bushwacker to murder him. He'd go after Jeremy White or one of the settlers because that was the reason the Association was bringing the assassin into the country. Clegg's fight with him was personal, so Clegg or one of his men would handle it.

When he reached Ed's place and dismounted, he was still uneasy. Rose was right about one thing. A single man had no chance against Clegg, and the trouble was that Jim, in a manner of speaking, was a man without a country. He couldn't with a clear conscience side with the settlers and he couldn't persuade any of the little ranchers north of B-in-a-Box to back him. None of them had any quarrel with the Association or Clegg. With them it was live and let live.

Jim yelled, "Ed."

No answer. Puzzled, he shoved the door open and looked into the shack. The bed wasn't made, dirty dishes were on the table along with a half-filled whiskey bottle. This wasn't like Ed. For a bachelor he had always been an unusually good housekeeper and Jim had never known him to drink alone.

He closed the door and walked to the barn. Ed's saddle horse was not in the barn or the corral. The saddle was gone, too. He must have decided to ride into town, Jim thought, although he had always waited before.

Jim mounted and rode toward Wheatridge, the uneasiness in him growing. In most ways he and Ed were completely different but they were alike in one way that was particularly important. Neither would run from a fight. Sam Clegg knew that, so the chances were that both were marked for death.

Another thing about Ed was the dismal fact that he was desperate. He had come here with a little money in his pocket, enough to put up a few poor buildings and buy a wagon and a team and the few odds and ends he needed to start his homestead. When Jim first met him, he spent hours telling about his girl back home, how pretty she was and what a good cook she was and what a wonderful woman she was.

Lately he hadn't even mentioned her. He had discovered something for himself that Jim could have told him in the first place, that you don't make any money out of a homestead when you start even if you have good land and plenty of water for irrigation.

By the time he reached Wheatridge, Jim knew he had to find Ed or he wouldn't sleep tonight. Something wasn't right, although he had no idea what it was. He tied in front of the Belle Union and went inside. Ed wasn't there. Jim made a methodical search of every saloon in town, but Ed wasn't in any of them and no one had seen him for a week.

Jim didn't find any Skull hands in town, and that seemed queer because Saturday night was the natural time for the whole crew to come to town. He did see several Rafter A punchers and a couple from Pitchfork and one from Wineglass. That was all. The town was abnormally quiet, and this added to Jim's uneasiness. Maybe he was boogery, but it seemed to him that everyone in town was just waiting for a blow up.

The last saloon he tried was the Palace. Doc Ashton and Larry Bain were here, and Jim joined them as soon as he had asked the bartender if he'd seen Ed Majors.

"I'll buy you a drink," Doc Ashton said amiably, "and then on the first of the month I'll send you a bill for patching you up the other day."

"Patching me up?" Jim turned to Bain. "What do you think of that, Larry? All he done was to punch and pull at me and ask me if it hurt and then tell me I was all right."

"I ain't surprised," Bain said. "It's the way a doctor makes money."

Ashton motioned at the barkeep who poured Jim's

drink and shoved it across the cherry-topped bar. Jim asked, "What's up? It's too quiet tonight."

Ashton and Bain exchanged glances, then Ashton said, "The word's out that the settlers are coming into town tonight loaded for bear. It's my guess Clegg doesn't want any trouble yet. He's probably holding back till the week's up, which is Monday."

Bain nodded. "He was in the store this afternoon. He told me he wanted to give the settlers every chance, that he didn't want trouble if he could help it."

"The pious egotist," Ashton muttered. "I hope somebody gets him mighty soon or he'll turn this valley red with blood. The man's a butcher."

Bain was usually not a nervous man, but he was nervous tonight. His hands trembled as he picked up his whiskey glass and drank, and the corners of his mouth were quivering. As he set his glass back on the bar, he said in a low tone, "Maybe I'll do it."

Jim stared at him, surprised. Larry Bain was no part of a fighting man. He was a storekeeper, he was honest, he gave more credit than a businessman should, and he asked for a fair profit and no more. He got along with everyone. For him to say a thing like that was so wild and incredible that Jim wondered if he had heard right.

"Go ahead, Larry," Ashton said. "Tell him."

Bain stared at his empty glass for a moment, then looked at Jim. "Sam Clegg has decided to get married again. He's picked Nora."

"Oh, come on, Larry," Jim said. "He's older'n you are. He knows Nora wouldn't take him."

"No, he don't know nothing of the kind," Bain said. "He always gets what he wants. You know that. He's got ways of twisting arms and pulling legs and hammering you over the head until you do what he wants." Bain shook his head. "No, he was dead serious. He stopped at the house and . . ."

A man poked his head through the door, calling, "They're coming."

Bain wheeled without finishing his sentence and

stalked out of the saloon. Ashton said gloomily, "He might do it. I've seen quiet men like Larry who can be pushed around, but they've got their limit the same as you do. When they reach it, they go crazy. If Clegg keeps at this, he'll push Larry right over his limit."

Ashton started toward the street door, Jim following. For Jim this was a night of surprises, and what he saw when he reached the street was almost as much of a shock as hearing that Sam Clegg wanted to marry Nora Bain.

A long line of horsemen was moving slowly along Main Street toward the courthouse. All of them carried Winchesters across their saddles, and all of them wore white sacks over their heads. Except for the eye holes, the sacks completely covered their faces.

A small man on a leggy black gelding rode at the head of the column. Back along the line was a bay with four white stockings. Ed Majors' horse! Jim rammed an elbow into Ashton's ribs. "That's Ed. Fifth one from the front."

"And that's Jeremy White leading them," Ashton said. "I told you he was as crazy and mean as Clegg."

"Maybe this proves he's as crazy as Clegg, but it don't prove he's as mean," Jim said. "We know their horses, so we know the riders. What do they think they're doing, playing some kind of game?"

"Looks like it to us," Ashton said, "but I don't think it's a game to them."

None of the riders looked to the right or left. They ignored the ribald remarks from the sidewalks. In spite of himself, Jim was impressed. Obviously Jeremy White meant for this to be a show of force that was intended to discourage Clegg, and he had disciplined the settlers so they kept the same pace and stared straight ahead.

Under other circumstances some of them would have exchanged insults with the crowd that lined both sides of the street. It was this discipline that Jim admired. Still, the white sacks over their heads made Jim think of a bunch of boys out on a Halloween lark.

When White reached the front of the courthouse, he

signaled for the men behind him to stop. He turned off the street and rode slowly across the weed-covered yard to the foot of the steps, his followers remaining in the street.

Dismounting, White climbed the steps and took a knife out of his pocket, opened a blade, placed a sheet of paper against the door, and drove the blade through the paper into the wood. He turned, came back down the steps, and mounted.

Now the farmers deliberately discarded the cloak of dignity with which they had entered town. White let out a rebel yell and dug in the steel. He rocketed across the courthouse yard as the riders in the street turned their horses and took up the yell. All dozen of them rode out of town on the dead run, firing their rifles at the sky and continuing to yell until they were out of Wheatridge.

Some of the people who had left the sidewalks to cross the street barely had time to get out of the way. Several fell in their wild scramble to escape the driving hoofs of the horses. After the settlers were gone, a sort of paralysis gripped the townspeople. Even the few cowboys in the crowd didn't say or do anything. To Jim the whole scene had been as wild and unexpected as a nightmare that scares a man and still somehow keeps him from waking up to realize it is only a nightmare.

"Farmers," Ashton muttered. "Riding plow horses. It wasn't possible, was it, Jim?"

"No, but it happened," Jim answered. "I've seen plenty of cowboys come into town the way these farmers left and scare hell out of people while they were doing it, but I'd like to know what White fed 'em to make 'em perform that way."

"You know," Ashton said thoughtfully, "I've got a hunch Sam Clegg is in for trouble."

Now the crowd had recovered. It streamed toward the courthouse. Buck Riley stood at the top of the steps staring at the sheet of paper White had impaled to the door.

Someone yelled, "What does it say, Buck?"

Riley yanked the knife from the door and turned to face the crowd, the sheet of paper in his hand. "It says for Sam Clegg and everybody who takes his orders to let the settlers on the Slow Water alone. It says they won't run. It's signed White Caps."

"Take it out to Skull," a man called. "Let Clegg read it."

"I'll do that," Riley said, and disappeared inside the courthouse.

The crowd drifted away. Jim and Doc Ashton stood on the corner, neither speaking for a while. Finally Ashton said, "I'm afraid to say what will happen next. I'm afraid to even guess."

"A few shots fired at that bunch of farmers might change things fast," Jim said.

"Maybe," Ashton said, "and then again, maybe not. I think they'll fight, partly because that man White is as tough as they come and some of it's bound to rub off on his neighbors, but mostly because they're like Larry Bain. They've got a limit."

"I still don't see the sense of wearing flour sacks over their heads," Jim said. "Makes 'em stack up like a bunch of school kids going to a masquerade party."

"White's got his reasons." Ashton scratched the back of his neck. "I don't have any idea what they are, but I'll bet you he's got them."

"Maybe he has," Jim agreed. "Well, I'd better slope along home and quit worrying about Ed. It looks like he's in good hands.

As he rode back to the B-in-a-Box, Jim found he couldn't quit worrying about Ed for the simple reason that wearing a white sack over his head and making a display of force did not protect a man from a drygulcher's bullet. On Monday morning, Jim told himself, he'd take the stage to Cheyenne.

11

The southbound stage to Cheyenne left Wheatridge at sunup, so Jim decided to stay in the hotel Sunday night rather than get out of bed in the small hours of the morning and ride to town. Before he left, he told Rose he was going to Cheyenne and would not be back until Wednesday evening, probably after dark. He asked if she wanted Ed Majors to come and stay at least during the nights.

She stared at him with loathing. "If that man comes around here while you're gone, I'll fill him full of buckshot. You'd better tell him."

Jim decided he had better see Ed and at least let him know he'd be gone for three days. Rose might do exactly as she said if Ed decided to ride to the B-in-the-Box to see him.

Rose hadn't said a word to Jim all day until she told him what she'd do if Ed Majors came around. She even refused to sit at the table with him. She'd been spiteful in various ways before, but this was the worst.

It was a sorry arrangement any way you looked at it, and Jim knew it could not go on. He didn't know why she was acting this way unless she thought he'd ride off and stay away if she was disagreeable enough.

The situation was bound to come to a head in a few days, he told himself glumly, although he couldn't see how his problem with Rose would be solved even when the bigger problem was worked out. He knew from long experience that even if Sam Clegg's power was destroyed, Rose would not forgive him, and he would be no closer to marrying Carrie than he was right now.

He found Ed sitting on his top step in front of his doorway. He hadn't shaved, he was bleary-eyed, and

Jim guessed the whiskey bottle he had seen the evening before on the table was empty.

He said, "How are you, Ed?" and hunkered down in front of the house and rolled a cigarette.

"You can tell how I am by looking at me," Ed said.

He was thick-lipped, but he wasn't so drunk he didn't know what he was saying. Jim said, "I never knew you to drink alone, boy. What's got into you?"

"Why shouldn't I drink alone?" Ed asked. "Why shouldn't I take my gun and blow my damned brains out if I've got any."

Jim struck a match, held the flame to his cigarette, and blew the match out. "Well, if you don't know, I sure can't tell you. I stopped last night. You weren't here."

"You know where I was," Ed said waspishly. "I seen you standing on the street with your town pals. You were looking at us like you thought we was fools."

"Yeah, I seen you, all right," Jim said. "You and your friends looked good, wearing them flour sacks and calling yourselves White Caps. What the hell is all that rigamarole going to get you?"

Ed chewed on his lower lip a moment, staring at Jim as if he wasn't sure whether Jim was asking a serious question or not. Finally he said, "It's Jerry White's idea. The only reason I ain't just walked off and left this stinking place is that I want to see Sam Clegg knocked on his butt. I've got a hunch Jerry can do it. He's a tough one. I never guessed how tough."

"Well, what is the reason for the get-up you were wearing?"

"You knew who we were from the horses we were forking," Ed said, "but supposing we swore somebody stole our horses and rode 'em to town to do something bad like maybe lynching a man. Even if you were right there watching the hanging, could you swear I was one of 'em doing it if you couldn't see my face?"

"Sure I could," Jim said. "It's loco to figure out a shenanigan like that. I know how big you are. I know how you sit your saddle. I knew who you were whether I could see your ugly mug or not."

"Sure," Ed agreed, "but remember we was riding slow and there was plenty of light on the street. Now suppose we came in fast and it was full dark off Main Street somewhere, do you still say you could swear it was me riding that bay of mine?"

Jim scratched his head and nodded. "Maybe White has got an idea at that, but just who are you figuring on lynching?"

"If Clegg brings in a killer and he plugs one of us, we'll hang him if we have to take him out of jail. Maybe we'll lynch Clegg from the same limb."

Ed rubbed his hands against his face, making a sandpapery sound. "It's a good feeling standing up on my hind feet, Jim. I never ran from a scrap, but then I never won a fracas, neither. We may get rubbed out, some of us anyway, but the rest will be there at the finish. It's a way Jerry White's got with me. Nobody's gonna run. Sam Clegg's gonna be one surprised cowman."

"Looks to me like you'd better stay sober," Jim said.

Ed lowered his head to his knees and didn't say a word. After a long time he spoke. "Jim, I came here with a big old dream about owning land and getting married and raising a family. Now by God, look at what's happened? My money's gone. I can't raise enough of a crop this year to do any good. There ain't much work around here. I can't send for my girl to come here and starve with me. I'm the worst kind of failure. I've got nothing. Nothing but a busted dream."

Jim finished his cigarette and flipped the stub away. More homesteaders had wound up with a busted dream than had ever made the grade. It was too bad Ed hadn't figured that out sooner. But he hadn't, and now he was close to panic.

"One thing I can't figure," Jim said. "You've been here more'n a year, but you've just now seen how things stack up. Why?"

"I guess I kept on dreaming," Ed answered, "but mostly

it's seeing Jerry White's fine place and his two hired men. He's making money. Good money. Some of the others have been here two years, a few of 'em three, and they'll have a crop this summer. They've got enough to fight for, but me, I've got nothing and I tell you my money's gone. What am I gonna do?"

Jim rose. "I'm going to Cheyenne in the morning to see the governor. I figure it's a wild goose chase, but it's worth a try. I'll be back in town Wednesday night. You hang on till then. We'll figure something out."

Ed looked at him, tears starting to run down his cheeks. He tried to say something, but all he could do was to swallow. The words didn't come. Jim slapped him on the back and mounted and rode away. He wasn't sure he had done right to hold out a slim hope, and only a miracle would keep the hope from being a false one.

Jim knew that Ed could not go to the bank and borrow a cent, partly because he had no collateral, or very little, but mostly because the bank wouldn't loan to a homesteader for the simple reason that Sam Clegg wouldn't like it. Jim also knew that he couldn't borrow anything from the bank to help Ed because Rose would have to sign the note with him and she wouldn't do it.

By the time he reached Wheatridge, Jim was sorry he'd mentioned the matter to Ed. Maybe he shouldn't even have stopped. The one possibility was to borrow a few dollars from Doc Ashton or Larry Bain. They were the only ones who might have enough guts to buck Clegg.

In the end Ed would still fail because it would take two more years to get his homestead shaped up to make a living on it, and neither Ashton nor Bain had that kind of cash to loan. Ashton was careless about collecting from his patients, and Bain carried so much on his books that he usually had to borrow from the bank to even stay in business.

Jim left his buckskin at the livery stable, took a room in the hotel, then went downstairs for supper. He studied the menu, ordered steak, and had just settled down with a bowl of soup when Nora Bain slipped into the dining room and took a chair across from him.

Surprised, he said, "Howdy, Nora. I didn't expect to see you."

She leaned forward, then glanced out of the window, and brought her gaze back to Jim's face. She was trembling and her face had turned pale, almost gray. She leaned farther forward so her motuh was as close to his ears as it could be.

"Carrie's staying with me," Nora whispered. "We saw you ride into town and she sent me to find you. Wait till dark, then come to the back door. She'll be waiting out there for you somewhere. Under the weeping willow or back of the woodshed. Stay there until she finds you and don't make any noise."

She rose and walked swiftly out of the dining room as if hoping nobody had seen her talk to Jim. He stared at her back, a dozen questions racing through his mind. One thing was sure. Nora had been too scared to stay long enough to give him any answers, and Carrie had been too scared to come at all.

12

Jim waited until it was black dark. The sky was covered
by storm clouds that had moved down from the Laramie
range so that even the starshine was blotted out. Light-
ning flickered and died above the mountains and the
rumble of distant thunder came to him as he walked
along the alley.

When he reached the back of the Bain house, he
turned along the side of the barn until he came to the
corner. He paused, his eyes probing the darkness, but
he did not see Carrie, and he hesitated to call to her.
Nora simply had not told him enough.

The back of the house was dark, but light fell through
the parlor windows in the front. Somebody was there
and Jim wondered if Sam Clegg was calling on Nora tonight. That could be the reason she had been so terrified.
She wouldn't welcome Clegg's advances, but she'd be
afraid to come right out and say so.

He heard Carrie's whisper, "Jim."

Relieved, he whispered back, "Here."

She darted toward him from the deep shadows of the
weeping willow in the opposite corner of the yard. "Oh,
Jim." She hugged him, then raised her hands to the back
of his head and brought his face down for her kiss.

When she drew away, he took a long breath. "Well,
honey, that kiss was worth waiting for."

"Even after this week and what they did to you?"

"I'm almost over that," he said. "One thing's sure.
They'll never catch me that way again."

"Jim, Jim, I've hated myself all week for getting you
into that," she whispered. "I didn't know they were trailing me. I knew Pa was bad, but I couldn't make myself
believe he was that bad. Now he wants to kill you."

"How'd you find all this out?"

"I kept on listening at keyholes," she answered. "I heard Pa talking to Lund and Manders that evening. Pa's never been careful about things like that. He doesn't think anyone would turn against him or desert him. He doesn't even think anybody would oppose him except you. He's going to fire Porter when his business with the settlers is over. He told Lund and Manders he'd pay them five hundred dollars to kill you. That's why I sent Nora to tell you to come here tonight. You've got to leave the country."

"I told you before I can't do that," he said.

"Well, at least you can go up into the mountains for a few days," she urged. "Just for a little while till things cool down. That's all I'm asking."

"No."

"Oh, you are so stubborn," she said angrily. "Don't you understand? I've left home. I don't have a home and I won't have till we're married. I'm living with Nora. I couldn't live out there after what happened."

He had wondered for a long time how she had been able to live with her father on Skull as long as she had. To him it seemed like hell at its worst. Now he said, "Of course you couldn't."

"I didn't even tell him good-bye," she went on. "I just left a note telling him I was leaving home and packed a few things and rode to town. I don't have any money and I don't have enough clothes, but I'll never go back, Jim. Never."

He backed up and leaned against the wall of the barn. Money, he thought glumly. Everybody needed money. Ed Majors. Carrie. Larry Bain, too, or soon would if Nora refused to marry Sam Clegg.

"What are you going to do?" he asked.

"I don't know," she said. "I just don't know. Pa's in the house now courting Nora. That's why I wanted you to come through the back this way. I didn't want you to run into him. It'd just make trouble and wouldn't do any good."

"Nora won't marry him, will she?"

"Of course not," Carrie answered. "He's an old fool to think she'd marry a man his age and an ornery one at that, but he never expects anybody to say no to him, so he thinks that if he goes through the motions of courting Nora she'll be happy to marry him."

"He can bring a lot of pressure on her."

Carrie was silent for a moment, then she said reluctantly, "I shouldn't have answered you the way I did. I should have said of course she wouldn't want to and she wouldn't be happy, but she might for her father's sake. You're right about pressure. You can guess what will happen if she turns him down and she can dangle him only about so long. He's already set the date. September first, he says, if it suits her. So far she's been able to keep from giving him a direct answer."

"Does he know you're here?"

"No. I've stayed inside the house since I came, but I can't go on doing that and having Nora take care of my horse and loan me clothes and feed me. I can sponge off her for a while, but I can't go on doing it."

Money, he thought again. If he just had a few dollars, enough to send her away so she could live somewhere else, maybe in Cheyenne, until he could send for her. But to marry her and take her to the B-in-the-Box to live with Rose . . . No, that was the one thing he could not let her do.

"I don't suppose you could get a job here in town," he said.

"I couldn't hold it if I did get it," she said. "I'd be fired as soon as Pa got the word to whoever I was working for." She gripped his arms. "Jim, we've got to get married. It's the only way out of this."

"Honey," he said, "I'm taking the stage to Cheyenne in the morning. I'll be gone three days. I'm going to see the governor and tell him what's happening here. He could put a stop to it if he believes me, though I doubt that he will. When I get back Wednesday, we'll figure something out. You can go on this way for three more days."

He thought, *I told Ed the same thing.* Was he a fool,

putting things off when they would be no nearer a solution than they were now? He waited, her hands still clutching his arms.

"Yes," she said in a low tone, "I can stand it for three more days. Will you marry me then?"

His first impulse was to say no, then he told himself they were already past the point of no return. They might just as well face that fact. Maybe Sam Clegg would think twice before he made a move against Jim and the B-in-a-Box if he knew it was his son-in-law he was attacking. Nothing would be lost if Clegg didn't think twice. Jim knew that if he kept putting Carrie off, he was bound to lose her.

"There's one thing I never told you," she said. "It's one reason I want to get married now. Pa has plans for me. He won't tell me just what they are, but he's talked about living in Cheyenne this winter and having me keep house for him. He wants to entertain and I'd be his hostess."

"It's no secret he has political ambitions," Jim said. "That was part of the plan when he put Dad in the legislature."

"That's right," she agreed, "so I have an idea he'll bargain me off as a wife to whoever will promise him the most. I know it sounds ridiculous, but a lot of the things Pa does sound ridiculous when you talk about them. For some reason they don't sound that way when he talks about them."

Jim took a long breath. "All right, we'll get married after I get back Wednesday. I can't take you home, though. I wouldn't put you through even one day of living in the same house with Rose."

"No, I don't want to," she said. "I may be dreaming, but I hope that after we're actually married, Pa will accept it."

"You are dreaming," he said.

"I . . . I guess so," she said wearily. "It's just that I can't go on this way, Jim. Anybody can stand so much worry and trouble and then something happens. Something's happening to me. It's like blowing air into a balloon and after while you know you can't put any more in without having it explode."

"Yeah, I feel the same way," he said. "Well, I'd better get back to the hotel."

He kissed her and she clung to him, not wanting to let him go. Later, when he was in bed in the hotel, he thought of what she had said, about standing just so much. She didn't realize it, of course, but the truth was she was only one of many who felt that way.

All of them were holding their balloons, and Sam Clegg kept right on blowing more air into each of them.

13

On Monday morning Jim boarded the stage to Cheyenne, arriving too late to see the governor that day, so he took a room in the hotel. He woke early from habit, shaved and dressed and had breakfast. After that he prowled streets until nine o'clock, then walked to the statehouse.

The secretary who had a desk in the outer office looked him over as if he were some kind of strange creature and an inferior one at that. He was a very thin man with a sharp nose that held a pair of pince-nez glasses. When Jim said he wanted to see Governor Farrel, the man took the glasses off his nose and continued to study him, his nose curling as if a bad smell had just come to him.

"Damn it, I want to see the governor," Jim said. "Tell him it's Jim Baron."

"Do you have an appointment?" the secretary asked.

"No. I came down on the stage from Wheatridge and I have to go back in the morning. The only reason I had for coming to Cheyenne was to see the governor."

"Impossible," the secretary said. "If you don't have an appointment . . ."

"Friend, I aim to see the governor." Jim put both hands palm down on the desk top and leaned forward. "I told you my name is Jim Baron. My father was Hank Baron. The governor and him was friends. He'll see me."

Obviously the name Hank Baron meant nothing to the secretary. He shook his head. "I'm sorry, Mr. Baron, but without an appointment . . ."

"If you don't ask the governor if he'll see me," Jim said softly, "you will be a hell of a lot sorrier."

The secretary leaned back in his chair. "Are you trying to intimidate me?"

"I'm not just trying," Jim said, "I'm doing it. I'm telling you to ask the governor to see me or I will twist your scrawny neck. It's a sorry situation when I pay taxes that goes for the salary of a pip-squeak like you."

The secretary rose. He was a tall man who seemed to keep unfolding until he stood a good six inches above Jim and now stared down on him. His black suit was carefully pressed, looking as if it had just that morning come from the cleaners.

"Governor Farrel is a very busy man . . ." the secretary began.

Jim started around the desk. The secretary cried out, "All right, all right. I'll ask him. You said your father's name was Shank Sharon?"

Jim's hands clenched as he fought his temper. He said, tight-lipped, "Hank Baron."

"Oh yes, Hank Baron," the secretary said, and disappeared into the governor's private office. He returned a moment later, saying stiffly as if he didn't believe it had happened, "The governor will see you now."

Jim strode past the man into the governor's office. Farrel stood behind his desk, a big hand outstretched. "Well, Jim Baron," he boomed. "The last time I saw you I reckon you were a little shorter than knee-high on a grasshopper. How are you, son?"

"I'm fine, Governor," Jim said, pleased by the greeting and surprised that Governor Farrell had ever seen him. "How are you?"

"Salty," the governor answered testily, "with a sore butt just from sitting. I'm getting damned tired of riding this chair behind a desk. If it wasn't for getting back home once in a while and forking my old paint horse, I'd lose what little savvy I had to begin with." He sat down and motioned to a chair. "Get a load off your feet, boy, and tell me what's on your mind."

Jim dropped into the chair, thinking that Governor Farrell was about as different from his secretary as it was possible for a man to be. His black broadcloth suit looked as if it had never been pressed and Jim thought it very likely it hadn't been since Farrel had bought it. The governor had deep lines around his eyes and down his cheeks, etched there by wind and sun, his face was darkly tanned except for a white line around his forehead where his hat protected him from the sun.

"It looks to me," Jim said, "as if the time you've spent riding that chair ain't changed you much."

Farrel laughed. "I don't aim for it to, neither. I'm a cowman just like Hank was, and Sam Clegg, and that's the way I aim to stay. Sometimes I wonder why I ever got into politics. I'll tell you one thing, though. I'm not staying in politics."

He picked up a box of cigars and held it out to Jim who took one, then he picked one up and bit off the end. "How is old Sam? He's a neighbor of yours if I remember right."

Jim nodded as he lighted his cigar. This was going to be harder than he had supposed, and suddenly he had a feeling he was destined for failure before he even started. He said, "Sam's fine, but we're headed for trouble. That's why I came to see you."

"Trouble?" Farrel laughed shortly. "I'm surprised. Old Sam was always a man who could handle any kind of trouble. Of course I haven't seen him for a long time, but I didn't figure he'd ever change."

"He hasn't," Jim said. "The truth is he's the cause of the trouble. You see, we have a few families of settlers who have moved onto the Slow Water below us. Just nine or ten altogether. They started coming in about three years ago. Sam didn't say nothing when the first family came, but two or three more moved in the second year, and then last year another five or six came. Now Sam has warned them to leave."

Farrel shrugged. "He's a patient man, son. I'm not real sure I'd have bothered to warn them. I know the problem. A cowman has to protect himself. You've got a good sheriff up there. Riley, isn't it? Buck Riley?"

Jim nodded. "I know the problem, too. So does Riley. Sam claims the settlers are stealing him blind, but I haven't lost any cattle and I don't believe Sam has lost enough to amount to anything."

Farrel's dark face tightened. "You say *Sam claims*. I don't like the way you put that, son. Now it's my feeling that if Sam Clegg *claims* he lost cattle to those nesters, that's exactly what he did. If the sheriff can't protect a man's property, then he's got to protect it himself."

"But not the way the Association is planning," Jim said. "That's why I'm here. I thought you might be able to head off the trouble. Riley can't. Or won't. The townsmen are caught in a bind and won't do anything. I don't know what I can do. Or any of the other small outfits. I belong to the Association, but I've got only one vote. The other little fry north of me don't even belong."

Farrel shook his head, the good nature gone from his face. "I don't have either the power or the inclination to step into a local problem. I think your sheriff can handle whatever trouble there is. Now if you'll excuse me . . ."

Jim rose and stared down at the governor. "I still haven't told you why I'm here. The Association plans to bring in a professional killer to murder a few settlers so the rest will leave. He may be there already."

Farrel's mouth dropped open. "I don't believe it. Were you at the meeting of the Association when they voted to do that?"

"No sir, but the information is correct."

"Who gave you this information?"

Jim hesitated, thinking he couldn't tell the governor or anyone else that Sam Clegg's daughter had been listening at keyholes. He shook his head. "I'm sorry, sir, but I can't tell you that."

"Well then, you shouldn't expect me to believe it." Farrel rose, so angry he was trembling. "If I were you, boy, I'd be careful about the gossip I carry. Good day."

"You can't just let a situation like this . . ."

"I respected your father," Farrel said, anger honing a fine edge to his voice. "I liked him as a man, but it doesn't always follow that a son takes after his father. I happen to know that Sam objects to the attention you've been paying his daughter. I consider this an effort on your part to discredit Sam. I will have nothing to do with it. Now you will leave or I'll have you thrown out."

For a moment Jim faced the governor, surprised that he knew about the relationship he had with Carrie and Sam Clegg's feeling on the matter, and he realized how Farrel, believing in Clegg, would look at the information he had brought.

There was nothing to do but turn around and walk out.

14

Four passengers besides Jim were on the stage when it left Cheyenne early Wednesday morning northbound for Wheatridge. Jim was sour-tempered because he hadn't slept much the night before and he'd drunk too much in the hotel bar. He felt like a failure, but when he thought about it, he didn't know what more he could have done.

The governor had turned hostile as soon as he heard why Jim was there. Hank Baron would never have done what Jim had. Neither would Governor Farrel, and he did not understand why Jim had come to him. It was treason the way he looked at it because Jim's interest and loyalty should have been with Sam Clegg and the Cattlemen's Association.

Even though he was grumpy, Jim introduced himself to the woman and the boy who rode beside him. She looked familiar, but he didn't place her until she said she was Mrs. Jeremy White and the boy was her son Tad. They had been in Cheyenne for some time, the boy needing treatments that Doc Ashton could not give him in Wheatridge.

"Well, I'm a neighbor of yours," Jim said. "Close enough that we should have met. The B-in-a-Box belongs to me and my sister Rose. We're on the North Fork upstream from Ed Majors' place."

"Of course," she said. "I should have recognized you. I've seen you in town."

"I seen you ride that big old sorrel horse of Clegg's last Fourth of July," Tad said eagerly. "It sure was a good ride. I guess nobody else could stay on him."

"I *saw* you ride, not I seen," his mother corrected patiently.

Irritation stirred in the boy's pale face, but he said nothing. Jim held out a hand to the well-dressed man who sat in front of him. "I'm Jim Brown," he said, "of the B-in-a-Box on the North Fork of the Slow Water."

"I'm pleased to meet you," the man said. "I may be visiting you one of these days. My name's R. C. Dillon. I represent the Rocky Mountain Land Development Company in Denver. The company's interested in putting in an irrigation project on the Slow Water, so it sent me up here to see what can be done."

"Now ain't that just fine," the man sitting beside him said. "Ain't that just dandy. My friend, Sam Clegg, is the big push up here on the Slow Water and he sure don't like dirt farmers. He likes land speculators even less. Ain't that right, Baron?"

Jim extended his hand. "That could be," he said. "I guess you heard my name."

The man nodded. "I'm Pete Hammer. Yes sir, I heard your name. And the lady's and the boy's name." He tipped his hat to Mrs. White. "Pleased to meet you, ma'am. You, too, Tad."

"I'm happy to know you, Mr. Hammer," Mrs. White said.

"So'm I," Tad said, and held out his hand.

Hammer took it, grinning. "Sonny, you're a man. Not many boys your age will shake hands without being asked. Now maybe I'm wrong, but I judge you live on a farm, Mrs. White. I happen to know that most folks on the Slow Water are farmers. Percentage would say that's what you was."

Mrs. White frowned. She glanced at Jim and then brought her gaze back to Hammer. "Yes, we live on a farm a few miles down the river from Mr. Baron."

She was a fine-looking woman, expensively dressed in a brown traveling suit, and Jim sensed that she had felt uneasy.

For several minutes there was a strained silence while the coach wheeled directly north over the rolling, grass-covered hills. Dust made a long, low cloud that hugged the earth for a time before it settled back to the ground. A wind would likely spring up later in the day, Jim thought, but for the time being, with the sun a bright orb above the eastern rim of the prairie, the air was almost motionless.

Jim brought his attention back to the men who sat across from him. He wasn't sure of his judgment of either. R. C. Dillon was about thirty, handsome, clean-shaven, and wearing a black derby on the back of his head and a brown broadcloth suit. A gold chain was stretched across his vest, an elk tooth dangling from it.

Apparently Dillon was not armed. At least no gun was in evidence. Pete Hammer was something else. He was older than Dillon, Jim thought, probably in his middle thirties, although it was hard to tell for sure because he had a sprinkling of gray at his temples and deep lines in his leathery face which was darkly tanned from years of exposure to wind and sun.

Hammer wore range clothes, clean enough, but far from new. His Stetson was battered and sweat-stained, his boot heels were run over, and even his calfskin vest showed wear. He could be a cowboy, a cattle buyer, or a guide of one kind or another. Too, he could be the killer the Association had sent for.

He wore a gun in a holster that hung from a cartridge belt. The holster was tied down in the manner of a professional gunman, but that proved nothing in this country. Jim had seen plenty of drifting cowboys who wore their holsters tied down in exactly that same way.

Hammer had a Winchester in the seat beside him, and he had brought a saddle and a warbag. Apparently he wanted to be considered a cowboy, but whether it was the truth or not was a question that plagued Jim. He realized that his uneasiness might have sprung from his knowledge that a killer had been sent for. Still, he could not put his suspicion out of his mind.

Tad was the first to break the silence. "Mamma don't like to be called a farmer. She never lived on a farm till we came to Wyoming."

"No offense, ma'am," Hammer said. "It's just that I've heard about the situation up here. You know, the settlers on the Slow Water on one side, and Sam Clegg and the Association on the other. They're fixing to run the settlers off their land, but of course you know all about that."

"No, I don't. I've been away." Mrs. White turned to Jim, her face turning pale. "Is that the truth, Mr. Baron?"

Jim had no intention of being drawn into the discussion, but the question was direct and he didn't know how to avoid answering it. He hesitated, then he said, "There has been some talk about it."

"You bet there has," Hammer said. "I figure to get a job with Clegg. Not that I've got anything against the settlers, ma'am, but I just kind of drift anywhere I smell a range war. The big cow outfits like Skull pay good and don't expect much work when they're paying fighting wages."

"I wouldn't be proud of it if I was you," Dillon said sharply. "I never have been able to understand how a man who is probably a fair hand would purposely get involved in a range war just because of the wages."

"Hell's bells," Hammer said as if he were insulted. "I suppose wages don't interest you one damn bit."

Dillon laughed shortly. "I don't say that, my friend, but my salary does not include going around shooting people I never saw before and have no reason to shoot."

"If the boss says to shoot 'em, I've got reason to shoot 'em," Hammer said. "No offense, ma'am." He nodded at Mrs. White. "You see, this here country is cattle range and farmers just don't belong on it. You ask the governor or anybody else that amounts to anything in Wyoming and they'll tell you the same thing."

Jim glanced at Mrs. White who was staring at Pete Hammer as if she considered him some kind of a vicious animal. She said nothing, but Tad burst out, "I think you're a real bad man, Mr. Hammer. I know some cowboys like Jim Baron, and I never heard one talk like you're talking."

"Oh, I don't usually talk this way," Hammer said. "Fact is, I ain't even sure what started me except that I got to thinking about Dillon here going to the Slow Water to look into some land development scheme. I'll bet Sam Clegg runs him out of the country the first day he's there."

"I don't think so," Dillon said, smiling. "I expect to stay at Skull while I'm looking around. I wrote to Mr. Clegg and he didn't show any hostility in the letter he wrote to me inviting me to stay on his ranch. You see, my company plays the percentages. We wouldn't do anything Mr. Clegg objects to. It's been my experience that cowmen don't fight the settlers if they can control the people who come in, or at least control the places where they settle. In fact, the arrangement can be an equitable one, with the farmers raising the hay the ranchers need."

Hammer snorted. "I want to see any cowman get friendly with a bunch of farmers or a land speculator, either. What you're saying is just a lot of hogwash."

"It's like the lamb and the lion, isn't it?" Dillon asked softly. "Well, my friend, it has been said that they will lie down together in peace."

After that the conversation lagged except for an occasional remark by Hammer. Jim, looking at one man and then the other, wasn't sure of either. The only thing he was sure of was the evident fact that Mrs. White was worried. He felt like smashing Pete Hammer across the mouth because there had been no reason for him to say what he had in front of Mrs. White.

When the coach made a noon stop at the Bard ranch, Mrs. White and Tad lingered until Jim caught up with them. Tad asked eagerly, "He was lying, wasn't he, Mr. Baron? That tough one named Pete Hammer was lying about Sam Clegg and the Association running us out of the country?"

He saw the questioning expression on Mrs. White's face. Again he didn't want to make a direct answer, but there seemed to be no way to avoid it. He said slowly, "It's like I told your ma in the stage, Tad. There's been a lot of talk about it, but I don't figure your dad and neighbors are going to be easy to run."

"You bet they ain't," the boy said. "You just bet your bottom dollar they ain't."

Mrs. White studied Jim as if she were making a judgment of him. Now she said, "Of course you are a cattleman, too, Mr. Baron."

She and Tad walked on toward the ranch house. Jim stared at their backs thoughtfully, telling himself that whatever happened would be hard on Mrs. White. He noticed that the boy was about as tall as his father. In another two or three years when he had his growth, he would probably be a head taller. He wondered how Jeremy White would accept a son that much taller than he was.

Later, when he caught Pete Hammer alone, he said softly, "Hammer, if you make one more remark in front of Mrs. White about Clegg and the Association chasing the settlers off the Slow Water, I'll make you pay for it when we get to Wheatridge."

Hammer stared at him in sheer amazement. "You?" he said. "Are you threatening me?" He laughed harshly. "Do you know who I am?"

"No, and I don't give a damn," Jim said. "Just remember what I said."

Hammer laughed again. "You scare me, Baron. You really scare me."

Jim walked past him toward the stage. He said nothing more. He had said enough, maybe too much.

But Hammer must have remembered the warning, for he didn't mention the matter again during the rest of the long ride to Wheatridge. Jim was relieved. There was no reason to worry Mrs. White about the settlers' problems. She would be worried enough when she got home.

15

The stage stopped in front of the Wheatridge hotel late in the afternoon, the sun hanging just above the Laramie range to the west. Jim was the first out of the coach. He turned, gave Mrs. White a hand, and then stepped back as Tad got down. R. C. Dillon and Pete Hammer followed.

Jeremy White was on hand to greet his wife, but his kiss was perfunctory. He patted Tad on the back absentmindedly, his gaze moving up and down the street. He said, "Get into the hotel, both of you."

Jim stared at him, amazed. White's tone was sharp, too sharp to greet a wife and son who had been gone for several weeks. When Mrs. White and Tad had disappeared into the hotel, Jim said, "What's wrong with you, White? You don't act as if you're very glad to see . . ."

"I've got all my boys in town," White interrupted. The stage had pulled away and was rumbling on down the street toward the terminal. "I think we can guarantee you a fair fight, Baron, which same is more than Buck Riley can do."

Now Jim was more than amazed. He was shocked. "What are you talking about? I'm not fighting anybody."

"You'll fight him or lie here in the street with his bullet in you," White said. "Check your iron. See that it's resting easy in leather. I don't figure he's fast, but chances are you're not, either. If he does put you down, I'll get him, though that ain't much comfort to a dead man."

Jim grabbed his arm. "White, are you going to tell me what in the . . ."

"Manders," White answered, his gaze whipping up and down both sides of the street as if he still wasn't sure who was there or how many there was. "The story I get is that the governor wired Sam Clegg you'd been to see him about the Association hiring an assassin to rub some of us out. I guess the governor wanted to know if there was anything to it. Kind of funny when you stop to think about it. The governor would know that Clegg wouldn't admit nothing of the kind. Anyhow, Clegg sent Manders to town to fix it so you didn't do no more talking."

Jim wiped his face with his right hand. It came away wet. He drew his gun, checked it, and eased it back into the holster. Sooner or later he would have called Dutch Manders and killed him. He'd promised himself that and had made no secret of his intention, so it wasn't any surprise to learn that Manders was in town to shoot it out with him. But for Jeremy White to be here siding him . . .

"Who are you, White?" Jim asked. "You're no more farmer than I am."

"Never mind who I am," White said. "Just be sure you take your time and put a slug into Manders where it'll do the most good. Six or seven Skull hands rode into town with him. They scattered. A couple of 'em are upstairs in the hotel. Two more are on the roof of the stable, so I'm guessing they never aimed for you to have a chance with Manders. Clegg's not a gambling man."

Jim had been staring at White, too shocked to grasp all that the man was telling him. Now he glanced along the street, and what he saw shocked him again. The crowd that usually met the stage when it arrived from Cheyenne was not to be seen. The only men in sight were White's friends, Ed Majors and Parson Bean and the rest of the farmers. Eleven of them. Every one carried a Winchester.

Jim wiped his face again. This was incredible. He didn't believe that White and his neighbors would accept him as an ally, but the fact remained that all of them had come to see that he had a fair fight, although Jim wasn't sure how White was going to manage it.

"You'll be facing the sun," White said. "It gives Manders the advantage." He took a long breath, his gaze on the batwings of the Palace. "I wish it was me. I know how

to handle these things, but I've done all I can for you."
He paused, and added, "Here he comes."

Dutch Manders had stepped out of the Palace. He
stopped in front of the saloon and pinned his eyes on
Jim, a big, formidable man, but Jim was not aware of
any feeling of fear. This was a moment he would have
brought about if Dutch Manders hadn't forced it sooner.

He had never seen Manders draw a gun, and he had no
illusions about his own speed. He had never seriously
practiced his draw, and to be a gunman you put in many
hours of practice. He suspected that Jeremy White had
done this and perhaps still did.

Now Jim was remembering that Dutch Manders had
held a gun on him that day on the North Fork while
Chick Lund and Bones Porter had beaten and kicked
him. This, to Jim's way of thinking, was not a mark of
courage, and it made Manders something less than a
brave man.

"I didn't think you figured we were on the same side,"
Jim said.

"I don't," White said. "You're a cowman and I'm a
farmer. By the very nature of things that puts us on opposite sides, but I believe in fair play." He grinned, glancing at Jim and quickly turning his eyes back to Manders.
"Besides, I don't want to miss a chance to cut Clegg
down a notch or two."

It was that, Jim thought, rather than White's belief in
fair play that had brought him and his neighbors to town.
But for the moment at least they were allies, and Jim
could be thankful for that.

Manders moved off the boardwalk into the street,
calling, "Baron, we heard why you went to Cheyenne.
That makes you a back-stabber. You ain't fit to be called
a cowman. Now get down and crawl out of town."

"One thing, Manders," White shouted. "The minute any
of your friends cut loose from the hotel or the roof of
the livery stable or wherever they are, you're a dead
man. This is between you and Baron and nobody else."

Jim was in the street now. He pulled his hat low over

his eyes to gain as much protection as he could get against the sun. He watched Manders closely, and it seemed to him that the man had not anticipated this development, even though he must have seen the settlers standing on both sides of the street with their Winchesters.

"I never figured it any other way," Manders said.

White snorted contemptuously. "You're a damned liar. If you do smoke Baron which I don't think you will, I'll take you on. You'll never ride out of town alive."

For a moment Manders stood motionless. Jim expected him to cave. No one on the Slow Water had ever seen Jeremy White draw a gun, but there were all kinds of stories about what the man had been before he came here. No doubt Manders had heard them, stories that ranged from claiming White had been a Texas Ranger to naming him a notorious gunfighter who had changed his name in the hope he could also change his life.

But Dutch Manders had gone too far to care. He said, "Give me an even draw. That's all I ask."

"It's all you'll get," White shouted back, "and it won't be enough."

Now Manders looked at Jim, his attention fixed on him as he pushed White out of his mind. He began moving toward Jim slowly, his shadow reaching far ahead of him. a long, dark shape on the dust of the street.

Jim said, "This is different from holding a gun on an unarmed man while two of your friends beat him up, ain't it, Dutch?"

Manders said nothing. He kept coming, right hand brushing the butt of his gun. Jim said, "It ain't too late to back out, Dutch. Get on your horse and keep riding. Don't ever come back."

Manders must have felt cornered, for suddenly he gave way to panic. He started to run toward Jim, yanking his gun from leather. He pitched three quick shots at Jim that were wild, then he must have realized how stupid this was. He stopped abruptly, his big legs spread. His gun had sagged in his hand. Now he tipped the barrel up again. Jim's Colt was leveled; Manders had given him ample time by panicking and now Jim pulled the trigger.

He felt the hard buck of the gun against his palm as powder flame lashed out from the muzzle of his .45, a bright tongue of fire in the long shadows that fell across the street. The sound of the shot was an echoing boom, thrown back by the false fronts, and echoing again. Manders never got off another shot. He was spun around and went down, his hat falling off his head and rolling away in the dust.

Jim paced slowly toward the man who lay on his face, his Colt in his hand, his eyes on the motionless figure. He saw one hand reach out toward the butt of the gun he had dropped, then go slack.

Now that the sound of the shooting had died, Jim was aware of the tense silence that gripped the town. Men stared from windows and doors, stared and did not move. They were frozen there, Doc Ashton and Larry Bain and Buck Riley and the others, frozen because Sam Clegg's man was dead. None of them knew what to do or make of it, or what would follow when Clegg heard.

Jim stopped two steps from Manders' body. He holstered his gun, certain that the man was dead. His nose was buried in the street dust, his outflung right hand was palm down, the tips of his fingers no more than an inch from the walnut butt of his gun.

This was the beginning, Jim thought. *Only the beginning.*

16

Slowly Jeremy White moved into the street to stand beside Jim. The other settlers followed, Ed Majors saying, "That was damned good shooting."

White nodded. "It sure was. Manders panicked like I figured he would. You had all the time in the world, Baron."

Jim didn't say anything. He kept looking down at Manders' body. He had never killed a man before and, although Manders deserved killing and Jim had every reason to kill him, the fact remained that he didn't feel good about it. He wondered if a man ever reached the point where a killing didn't hit him like this. Jeremy White would know, but Jim didn't ask.

"Let's get out of town," White said. "We'll stay out until Clegg makes his next move."

"He won't wait long," Ed Majors said.

"Then we'll be back." White wheeled away, jerking his head at the others. "Let's ride."

Now, as the farmers strode to their horses and mounted, the townsmen came into the street and crowded around Jim and the dead man. Doc Ashton knelt in the dust and turned Manders over on his back. The bullet had caught him in the center of his chest. He had not lived long after being hit.

Ashton felt for a pulse and rose. "He's dead." He stared at Jim as he chewed on his lower lip, then glanced at the farmers who were riding out of town. He said, "Somehow this isn't the way it's supposed to work. Homesteaders don't fight. They get killed or they run away, but White has turned these men into a wolf pack."

"Sure, but it was Jim who had the guts to fight," Larry Bain said. "Now what happens?"

Jim looked at the faces of the men who surrounded

him. He thought, *They're scared. They're so scared they don't know what to do.*

Ashton motioned to some men beside him. "Get that stretcher in my office. We'll move him off the street."

"Sam will hear what happened in about an hour," Bain said. "The other Skull men who were hiding on the roof of the livery stable and upstairs in the hotel got out of town the minute Manders went down."

Buck Riley had been there from the moment the townsmen had come into the street. Now he said harshly, "I want you out of town, Jim. Pronto. I won't be responsible for what happens to you after Clegg hears about this."

Then the anger and the contempt that had been rolling up in Jim could not be contained. He said coldly, "What kind of a sheriff are you, Buck? You weren't going to move a hand when those killers were fixing to smoke me down." He wheeled to face Bain. "You're no better, Larry. Or you, Doc. You've made some tough talk, but if it hadn't been for Jeremy White, I'd have fought Manders and I'd have caught a slug before he fired a shot."

Riley said, "I'll saddle your horse."

As the sheriff strode toward the livery stable, Bain called, "Fetch a pack horse, Buck." He turned to Jim. "You're going to have to get back into the mountains, Jim. Clegg will turn his whole outfit loose on you when he hears."

"That's right," Ashton said. "You can cuss us out till you're black in the face. We deserve it. We're a bunch of hot air merchants and I'm ashamed of myself, but the fact is we can't defend you and the settlers are gone. They won't want you holing up with them, either. You can't go home because Clegg will go there and burn you out if he finds you."

He was dead right. Jim knew it. Sam Clegg had just lost one of his best men. Dutch Manders had been with him for a long time. He was the kind of hired hand who would do exactly what he was told to do. Now Clegg would turn his revenge over to Chick Lund who would keep after Jim until he caught him and killed him.

"Come to the store and I'll give you all the supplies you need," Bain said. "You know those mountains like your own range. They'll never catch you once you get the bulge on them."

Jim nodded and turned toward the store. He was sick, not because he had killed a man and not because for the moment he was going to run, but because Doc Ashton and Larry Bain and the other townsmen he had thought of as friends wanted him out of town because he was a danger to them and the town as long as he was here.

He said nothing while the supplies were being piled on the boardwalk in front of the Mercantile and Riley had come with the buckskin and a pack animal. He saw Mrs. White and Tad drive by in a buggy they had rented from the livery stable.

R. C. Dillon and Pete Hammer had watched the fight from the hotel lobby. Now they left the hotel, Dillon looking at Jim with cold indifference. Hammer was carrying his Winchester, warbag, and saddle.

"We're renting a couple of horses and riding to Skull, Baron," Hammer called. "The next time I see you, I'll be working for Sam Clegg and you'll be a wanted man."

"And you'll be trying to collect the price that Sam puts on my head," Jim said.

"That's right." Hammer boomed a laugh. "I'll collect it, too."

They went on to the livery stable. Ashton asked, "Who are they?"

Jim told him as much as he knew, and Bain said, "You figure one of them is the killer who's supposed to show up here?"

"Maybe," Jim answered. "They didn't tell me."

As soon as the supplies were packed, Jim stepped into the saddle. Ashton was staring thoughtfully at the backs of the two men until they disappeared through the archway of the stable. He said, "The man who threatened you might be the one. He looks like a tough hand."

"If he is," Jim said, "he's the only one in Wheatridge."

"Oh, I dunno," Ashton said, grinning. "I'd say you qualify."

He could grin at what amounted to an accusation of cowardice, but Larry Bain and Buck Riley couldn't. Riley said, "Don't get smart, Jim. You played dumb going to see the governor. You can't blame Clegg for trying to rub you out. What did you expect to happen?"

"I expected a lot of things to happen that didn't," Jim said.

Larry Bain's face turned red. He said, "I guess maybe you've got a right to feel the way you do." He swallowed and looked away. "Last night Nora told me she couldn't marry Sam no matter what happened. She's going away. She doesn't know where."

Bain swallowed again and brought his gaze back to Jim's face. "Don't say what you'd like to. I've said it all to myself, but I still don't know what to do. I know Sam Clegg and I know what I'm capable of doing. I kept hoping all the time that something would happen that would change things, but it will take a miracle and I don't believe in miracles."

"I figured on seeing Carrie," Jim said. "Tell her what happened and tell her I ain't going to be gone very long."

"I'll tell her," Bain promised.

"You'd better be gone long," Riley said. "Looks like I know Sam Clegg better'n you do."

"I know myself," Jim said, "and I sure am getting acquainted with you boys."

He rode away, angling toward the B-in-a-Box. He had no intention of going very far into the mountains or staying away for more than a couple of days. A man never solved a problem that way, and this problem was one that would not wait. Still, he was no closer to a solution than he ever had been, but a day or two by himself might help him reach a solution. Then he laughed aloud. Sam Clegg was not likely to let him have a couple of days to himself.

He was sorry he didn't have a chance to see Carrie, but she would probably have insisted on coming with him if she knew. He was sorry, too, that he wasn't giving Ed Majors the help he had promised, but Jeremy White would see that Ed didn't starve.

By the time he could look down on the B-in-a-Box from the ridge top, the light had thinned and darkness was only minutes away. Rose had lighted a lamp. She would be expecting him to get back tonight, but there wasn't any point in stopping to talk to her.

He rode on, his thoughts turning to Jeremy White and again he wondered who the man was. He had, as Doc Ashton had said, turned the farmers into a wolf pack and that was quite a trick. Jim had not thought it was possible. One thing had come clear. Jeremy White was a man, just about the most man there was in Slow Water County.

By the time he reached the North Fork, the last hint of the flaming sundown had left the sky and darkness had settled down as the jaws of the canyon closed around him.

17

Sam Clegg stood stiffly in front of his ranch house, the riders who had left Wheatridge after Manders had been killed lined up before him. They had told him what had happened, emphasizing the fact that Jeremy White and his neighbors had been on the street, they were all armed, and any effort to cut Jim Baron down would have brought on a pitched battle, the one thing that Clegg had said to avoid. He hadn't wanted the town shot to pieces which would alienate the townsmen, and he didn't want to do anything that would force Buck Riley into the settlers' camp.

Clegg had listened. Now he was silent as he stared past his men at the ragged skyline of the Laramie range to the west. All the time that he had stood here listening to what had happened in Wheatridge, he'd had the strange feeling that this was a nightmare. It could not have happened. It was impossible. Dutch Manders couldn't be dead.

Most of his men were expendable. Manders wasn't. He had learned long ago that an order given to either Manders or Chick Lund would be carried out no matter how ruthless or brutal it was. But the fact was Manders was dead, a blow that was equivalent to losing his right arm.

"All right," Clegg said at last. "In the morning we'll decide how to play it."

The men didn't move. They looked at each other and shifted their bodies in the saddles. Finally the youngest man in the outfit, a fiery, impatient kid named Red Schone, said, "Boss, we don't think that's a good idea."

"Oh, you don't," Clegg said softly. "Now just what the hell would you do, Red?"

"We talked it over riding back from town," Red said. "We didn't cotton to the notion of tucking our tails be-

tween our legs and running home after that bunch of sodbusters had taken over the town. If we'd had our druthers,
we'd have cleaned their plow for 'em, but you gave
your orders . . ."

"All right, all right," Clegg broke in roughly. "I asked
you what you'd do about Jim Baron?"

"We want him," Red said, "and we figure that by morning he'll be fifty miles from here."

Clegg's smile was a wintry tightening of his lips. "You
boys don't savvy Jim Baron. I do. I've knowed him since
he was knee-high on a toad. He won't go far. Now go eat
your supper. We'll be moving out of here before sunup."

He wheeled and strode into the house, deep in thought.
What was the next step? The main thing was to make
each move carefully and thoughtfully and not take any
chances. He had thought he was not taking any chances
when he'd told Dutch Manders to go to town and take
care of Jim Baron when he stepped out of the stage, but
Manders was dead.

The one thing that Clegg had not foreseen was Jeremy
White's part in what had happened. How could anyone
have foreseen that even a hard case like Jeremy White
could weld a band of settlers into a wolf pack the way
White had done.

The housekeeper called supper and Clegg walked
back into the kitchen and sat down at the table and began to eat, his mind moving with cold precision to several
conclusions.

Number One. When Ace Alred's man arrived, he
would rub Ed Majors and Jeremy White out, and that
would be enough to break the back of the settlers.

Number Two. As soon as the settlers were gone, his
men would settle on the Slow Water. He would buy their
homesteads the day they proved up on them. In a few
years he would own all the good meadow land. (This
was something he should have done a long time ago, but
he'd neglected it, not thinking the settlers would ever be
the tough opponents they were turning out to be. But

again, how could he have foreseen that a man like Jeremy White would become a part of his problem?)

Number Three. Jim Baron had to die. Clegg had decided that several days ago when Carrie had left home. Carrie had chosen Jim Baron, and so now she was no longer Sam Clegg's daughter.

He finished eating and went back into the front room. He took a cigar from the box, bit off the end and fired it, then sat down in his black leather chair and mapped out his campaign for tomorrow. He'd have Baron before dark. He was sure of it.

First, Clegg eliminated the moves he was sure Jim wouldn't make. He would not stay in town. Buck Riley wouldn't stand for it and he doubted that the businessmen would, either, knowing how he would feel about it. Jim wouldn't try to hide out with any of the settlers, except possibly with Ed Majors.

Then Clegg looked at the other side. Jim might go home and wait for whatever was to happen. Clegg hoped he didn't because it would put Skull in a bad light if it attacked a man who was defending his own home.

The other possibility and it seemed to Clegg to be the best one was the chance that Jim would go up the North Fork and hide out for a while. He wasn't a man who would stay there very long, but it might be long enough for Chick Lund to hunt him down and kill him.

He knew, then, what he'd do. In the morning he'd take half of his crew and see if Jim was hiding on Ed Major's farm, then he'd go to the B-in-a-Box. He'd come home if he didn't find Jim in either place. Chick Lund was a good tracker who knew the mountains as well as Jim did. He had plenty of reason to rub Jim out. If he didn't, Jim would be on his tail and Lund knew it.

Clegg heard two men ride up and stop in front of the house. Clegg stepped outside. In the dusk light he could not make them out clearly, but he saw they were strangers. They dismounted, one of them coming to him, his hand extended.

"I'm Pete Hammer," the man said. "Ace Alred sent me."

"Good." Clegg shook hands, suddenly relieved because now the end was in sight. "I'm glad to see you, Hammer."

The other man stepped up and held out his hand. "I'm R. C. Dillon. I wrote to you about looking over the country with the idea of developing the land. With your permission, of course."

Clegg had almost forgotten about Dillon and the letter. He had consented to Dillon's coming because he had thought it would be a good gesture on his part to appear to encourage an irrigation project. That would make it seem that he was opposing the settlers who were now on the Slow Water only because they were the rustlers he accused them of being. Later, of course, he could always find a way to handle this man Dillon.

"I'm not sure anything will come of your project," Clegg said as he shook hands with Dillon, "but you're welcome to stay and look around. Take your horses to the corral. I'll have my housekeeper fix supper for you."

Hammer and Dillon followed him into the house a moment later, Dillon glancing around the big room in frank admiration. "You have a fine place here, Mr. Clegg." He studied Napoleon's portrait, and added, "I would guess you and I share admiration for Bonaparte. A truly great man, Mr. Clegg. Not only in war, but in many of the arts of peace, also. His legal code, for instance."

"Yes, a great man," Clegg agreed. "Well, I expect both of you are hungry. My housekeeper, Mrs. Horn, has set a snack on the table for you. Go ahead and eat, then I want to talk to Hammer. Dillon, I expect you're tired and will want to go to bed."

"It's been a long day," Dillon agreed. "I don't know of anything that's more tiring than riding a stage."

Clegg stared thoughtfully at the backs of the men as they went into the kitchen and sat down. Hammer was carrying a revolver and had come in with a Winchester which he had leaned against the wall beside his warbag.

You never know the caliber of a man until you see him

in action, but over the years Clegg had learned to trust his reaction to a stranger when he first met him. He had a feeling that Hammer looked the part, but he wasn't tough enough to do what he was hired to do.

Hammer had the appearance of a drifting cowhand and Clegg had seen dozens of them come and go. On the other hand, Dillon who was dressed like a dude and apparently wasn't even armed, had the cold, pale eyes of a killer.

Dillon was a good-looking man, pleasant and polite with a talent for saying the right words, but Sam Clegg had never known a man who had the dead-fish expression in his eyes that Dillon had who wasn't capable of killing a man with as little feeling as you would have knocking over a prarie dog. Clegg sighed, wishing the two men were reversed, but Ace Alred probably knew what he was doing when he'd hired Pete Hammer.

When the two men came back into the front room, Hammer said, "We rode up from Cheyenne with Jim Baron. We saw him gun your Dutch Manders down. I told him the next time I saw him I'd be working for you."

Clegg felt his belly muscles tighten. He said uneasily, "You shouldn't have told him that. I didn't aim to advertise it."

Hammer shrugged. "No sense hiding the truth. I aim to hang around town for a few days and sort of get the lay of the land. When I move, I'll move fast and good."

"We'll talk in a minute." Clegg turned to Dillon. "I'll show you your room. One thing you should know. We're having a little trouble on this range, so it may be dangerous for you to ride around alone."

"I can take care of myself," Dillon said. "Now I have some information that may interest you. I saw a man in town today who goes by the name of Jeremy White. That's not his real name. I have an idea he came here to hide out. He's a gunfighter named Keno Ross. He made a fortune in a range war in Texas until he had to leave the country because he killed the wrong man. Coming up here and taking a homestead was the best kind of disguise."

Clegg might have known. Well, he did know that White was more than an ordinary homesteader, but he'd had no way to identify him.

"You're room is upstairs," Clegg said, and led the way.

When he reached the room, he lighted a lamp on the bureau and turned toward the door. Dillon said, "Don't be alarmed if I get up during the night. Sometimes I have trouble sleeping. When that happens, I like to take a ride."

"You may miss breakfast," Clegg said, and left the room.

He went down the stairs and, pulling out a drawer of the desk, picked up a map of the Slow Water Valley which showed the homes of the settlers. He said, "I assume that Ace made the proposition clear, one thousand dollars for each pelt you take."

"Agreed," Hammer said.

"Two will be enough, I believe," Clegg said. "Ed Majors, and then this man Jeremy White that Dillon was talking about."

"All right," Hammer said. "Now I think I'll go to bed. I'm like Dillon. Riding a stage all day is hard work." He picked up his Winchester and warsack, then he asked, "What about this man Baron?"

"We'll take care of him ourselves," Clegg said stiffly, and turned to the stairs.

Later, when he was in bed, he stared into the darkness, vaguely uneasy. He wasn't satisfied with Pete Hammer. He wasn't satisfied at all. The man had been a fool to announce in Wheatridge for everybody to hear that he was working for Sam Clegg.

Clegg's heart began to pound. He should never have trusted Ace Alred to hire Hammer. Tomorrow he would fire the man before it was too late.

18

Jim had no intention of going far or staying away more than two or three days. His flight would do two things, he thought. It would take the pressure off the townsmen and the settlers and Rose. Perhaps Clegg would make a superficial search for him, but he would soon guess that Jim had headed for the mountains. The second thing would be to bring Clegg or some of his men after him, and that was exactly what he wanted.

He rode up the North Fork only as far as the clearing where the Skull men had caught him and beaten him. They would naturally expect him to go higher into the mountains, and that would give him an advantage. He hoped that Chick Lund would be with the men who were pursuing him. His score with Lund was still not settled.

He unloaded the pack horse and built a fire, then staked both animals out behind a screen of willows. He cooked supper, threw more wood on the fire, and made his bed back of the clearing in the brush. He didn't expect the Skull men to show up before daylight, but he'd be ready if they did.

For a time he stayed awake, his Winchester beside him. The fire died down, but he did not build it up. The smell of smoke would linger for a while. They would know he had been here, but they would not know he was still here.

He heard the steady pounding of the creek, the rustle of some tiny animal darting through the dry leaves beside him. He stared at the clear sky and thought about the next moves he had to make.

He had taken care of Dutch Manders. The revulsion that he had first felt because he had killed a man was gone, but he didn't feel any satisfaction in what he had done, either. It had been forced upon him, and now, thinking about it, he wasn't at all sure he would ever have forced the fight if Manders hadn't jumped him.

He knew, too, that he would find no satisfaction in taking his revenge on Chick Lund and later in smoking Sam Clegg down, but there would be no peace on the Slow Water until Clegg was dead. When that happened, Ace Alred and the other members of the Association would sing another tune.

Funny about people, he thought. With Clegg gone, the rest of the cowmen would not make trouble. Buck Riley would be an adequate sheriff, and Doc Ashton and Larry Bain and the rest of the townsmen would all be good neighbors again. Without Jeremy White, the settlers would be nothing. Probably they would all have left the country before now if White hadn't been here to hold them together.

White and the settlers had saved his life, but this did not mean that any of them except Ed Majors had any regard for him. For a short time he had been useful, a fact that briefly had made allies of them.

In the end they would turn against him if they survived. As Mrs. White had said in the stage, he was a cowman, and in their eyes that kept him from being neutral. But again it all depended on who was alive when the fight was over. If Jeremy White was killed, Jim could get along with any of the rest who stayed.

Slow Water County was like a schoolroom, he thought. He remembered how it had been when he was a boy and had gone to school with the Riley kids and some of the other neighbors. One boy named Okie Pell was a little older than Jim and Buck Riley. He was a young hellion who could think up more deviltry in one day than the others could in the entire year. Hiding a skunk in a drawer of the teacher's desk was typical.

The main thing Jim remembered about those years in school was the good time all of them had when Okie was absent, and how he upset everyone when he was in school. Killing a man was a hard way to settle a problem, but Jim was convinced that this one had reached a point where a few funerals were a necessary requirement for peace.

Then his mind turned to his personal problem as it always did when he had time to think, of Carrie and himself and Rose. Rose, Rose, always Rose and her domineering ways.

Jim had said repeatedly that he would never ride off and leave the B-in-a-Box. He had put too much sweat and blood into it to simply walk off and leave it. Now, and this came to him as a surprise, he realized suddenly that was all he could do because he could not face the future without Carrie.

She had asked him to marry her and go away with her. Now he knew that was the only thing he could do and he wondered why he had been so slow to see it. Rose wanted the B-in-a-Box and she was as unchanging as these mountains. All right, he'd let her have it.

This decision brought a measure of peace to him that he had not felt for a long time. He had not intended to sleep, but he dropped off, then woke with a start, the first glow of dawn showing in the sky about the eastern ridge. For a moment he wasn't sure what had wakened him, then he knew. Horses were coming up the canyon.

Taking his rifle, he moved to the fringe of willows and waited, his heart pounding. The odds would likely be about six to one, and if Chick Lund was leading this bunch, which he probably was, he'd know that if he didn't get Jim, Jim would surely get him.

He had not expected them so soon, but he was glad they were coming. They were close now, so he'd soon have it over. From the sound of the shod hoofs on the rocky bottom of the canyon, he didn't think there were more than two or three horses and he did not understand that.

A moment later two riders appeared in the clearing below him. He did understand what was happening when he heard Carrie call, "Jim."

He scrambled through the brush toward them, cursing. He couldn't see who was with Carrie until he was halfway across the clearing and recognized Nora Bain. He stopped, so angry he knew he shouldn't say anything, but he couldn't hold back the words, "What in the hell are you two doing here?"

"We came to have breakfast with you," Carrie said. "Build a fire. Nora's dad said you had plenty of grub for all three of us."

They rode toward him. He didn't move. All he could think of was that he had to get them out of here before the Skull riders showed up. He couldn't think of anything that would work, not with Carrie.

"Jim, don't be mad at us," Nora cried. "It's my fault we're here. I was too afraid of Sam to stay home. The last time he came to see me, he said there wasn't any sense of waiting until September. He wants to get married in a few days."

"This is crazy," Jim said. "Some of Sam's men are bound to ride in here before long. If they find you two . . ."

"We thought of that," Carrie said as she reined up and dismounted, "so we didn't wait until daylight. We wanted to get here before they did. We both have rifles and we're good shots. We'll hide in the brush and fight with you. You'll need some help."

Nora was off her horse, too. She walked to Jim. "Don't send us back. I can't face it any longer. I could as long as I thought I had until September, but I can't now. I'd rather face death than to be forced to marry Sam Clegg."

"I knew you'd be here," Carrie said. "You never could make yourself run from anything. This is where they beat you, so this is where you decided to wait for them. We're not going back, so don't try to make us."

He wondered if all women were stubborn. He laid his rifle down and took Carrie into his arms. "I'll start a fire in a minute," he said, "but I want to tell you something. I just now got everything into focus. I guess I've had things stacked up wrong in my head because I kept thinking the B-in-a-Box was Number One. It isn't, you are, so if you still want to get married and go away, that's what we'll do."

"Oh Jim, I've wanted to hear you say that for so long," she said, and began to cry.

He held her in his arms, her face pressed against his chest.

19

When Ed Majors woke that morning, the early dawn light was showing in the east window. For a time he lay there, watching the light slowly deepen, and he thought glumly of the big dreams that had been his this past year, dreams he had passed on in his letters to his girl back home in Nebraska.

He had been a fool, a plain, pure, simple fool. Jim could have told him. In fact, Jim had tried to tell him, but nobody told Ed Majors. Of course, nobody told a fool, and that's what he was. He simply hadn't had enough money to hang on until he could make a living on his homestead.

He had supposed that all you had to do was to work hard, to put your plow into the ground and turn it over and harrow it down and seed it, then dig a ditch and take water out of the river and let it flow out across the field.

He was a dreamer, sure enough. He had not realized that there might be so much wet weather in the spring that he couldn't plow or harrow, but most of all, he had not in his wildest nightmares imagined how difficult it was to lay out a ditch that would put water on a field. If Parson Bean hadn't helped him, he never would have finished his ditch.

By the time he had water on the land, it was too late for a crop. The wheat looked fine for a while, then it turned yellow and died, and that was it. This year he couldn't even scrape up enough money to buy seed. He was whipped ten ways from Sunday and all of his dreaming and determination didn't change a thing.

He had worked hard. Usually he would have been up doing the chores before this, but now he had no incentive. He'd stay here until the fight with Sam Clegg was over with, then he'd head for Nebraska. They'd win it. That was something he had never really doubted. Jeremy White was a man who wouldn't settle for anything less than victory. Another day. Two days. It didn't take long when you reached this point, White had said last night when they'd got back from town.

Ed was out of money and whiskey, and he had nothing to eat except coffee and eggs. He might just as well start eating his hens. He wouldn't get much if he sold them. Anyhow, he'd have enough when he sold his saddle horse and team and milk cow to get back home. He'd find a job and tell his girl he was a big, fat zero. That would be the end of his romance. She could find plenty of men to marry who had something.

He would have stayed in bed, but he had to get up to relieve himself. Wearing only his drawers, he crossed the room to the door and opened it. The morning light was still thin, with a faint bank of fog lying along the creek. He took one step through the door when a rifle cracked from the willows, the bullet passing so close to the side of his head that it cut a few hairs.

The sheer instinct of survival sent him flat on his face and drove him back into the cabin, scurrying crab-like through the door until he had put a wall between him and the assassin. He lay flat on his belly, so scared he couldn't get a good breath. Jim's information about the Association sending for a killer was right, but why had he been picked for a victim? Maybe there was no reason except that he was Jim Baron's friend.

As soon as he recovered from that first paralysis of fear, he was furious. He crawled to the corner where he had left his Winchester, levered a shell into the chamber, and then stood up and edged toward the window. He couldn't see anyone, of course. A man who would try to pick you off this way wouldn't show himself.

Then, to his surprise, he did see someone. A man was riding downstream on the other side of the creek. He was too far away to identify, and in light as thin as this, it would be a waste of ammunition to shoot at him.

Ed moved to the door and watched the rider until he disappeared from sight. The fog was thicker downstream and seemed to swallow the man and horse. He wouldn't try for anyone else this morning, Ed thought. Not in broad daylight, anyhow. Tonight at dusk maybe, or in the morning.

He built a fire and dressed, then went outside and took care of his stock. Now that the danger was over, he began to sweat. His stomach felt as if it had collapsed against his backbone.

Ed had never considered himself a hero, but he had always given himself credit for average courage. It was just that being shot at by someone you never saw and therefore couldn't fight was enough to take the guts out of anybody. He'd be dead right now if the light hadn't been so bad. The fog had helped, too.

He set the coffeepot on the stove and started to fry two eggs when he heard a rifle crack from somewhere downstream. He stepped outside and cocked his head to listen, but he heard nothing more.

He went back inside, feeling vaguely uneasy. A little guilty, too, because he should have saddled up and ridden down to Parson Bean's place and warned him, but damn it, he had been so sure the killer wouldn't try again. Besides, why would he murder Parson Bean who was the kind of man who never harmed anyone?

Ed tried to assure himself that the Parson had seen a deer, but the uneasiness lingered. He finished breakfast, then decided he'd ride down to Bean's place and find out for sure about that rifle shot. He wouldn't breathe easy until he knew. If the Parson had been murdered, he'd never breathe easy again because he would always know he could have stopped it.

When he finished saddling his horse, he looked downstream and saw the smoke rising from the bluff north of the White farm. He knew then that the worst had happened. He got his rifle and flour sack from the house, mounted, and rode down the river, a little sick deep in his belly. The Parson was dead and he was to blame. Nobody had to tell him. He knew.

When he reached the Bean house, he saw that White's buggy was in front. The bigger children were sitting on the ground near the corral gate, all of them crying except the oldest boy who was about the age of Tad White.

Ed reined up. "What happened, Bud?" he asked.

"Pa's dead," the boy answered. "He went out to milk afore it was full daylight. He was halfway between the house and barn when somebody cut loose from the creek. Pa caught it dead center. He was gone afore any of us got to him."

"You see anyone?"

"No." The boy shook his head. "We were all too scared and everything. We didn't even look." He swallowed, then he said, "Mrs. White's inside with Ma and the baby. She said Mr. White, he says for you to come right on down to his place. They're fixing to go after the killer."

Ed nodded and rode away. He didn't want to think about what Jeremy White would say when he told him that he could have saved the Parson's life.

When he reached the White farm, he saw that almost all of the neighbors were there. The boy Tad was with the men, a rifle in his hands. Ed guessed Tad would be riding with the men and he didn't like it, but he wasn't one to argue with Jeremy White.

As he dismounted, he glanced around the circle of tight-lipped men. He discovered that one of the settlers, the man who lived the farthest downstream of any of them, was still missing. So was Tom Wheeler, one of White's hired hands.

No one wanted to talk. They stood holding their rifles, waiting. When Ed looked around the circle of faces, he felt as if he didn't know them. They were strangers, grim, angry, capable of anything. He knew, without being told a word of White's plan, that the killer wouldn't live five minutes if they caught him.

Ed let the reins dangle and crossed to where White

stood beside Tad. He said, "Jerry, I've got to tell you. I'm to blame for the Parson getting drilled the way he done. You see, this drygulcher tried for me first, but the light was too thin to shoot straight and there was a little fog that bothered him. He just barely missed me. I should have saddled up and warned the Parson, but I didn't figure he'd try anybody else. Not till dusk anyhow."

White nodded. He looked at Ed and then looked away, a strange expression in his eyes. He said, "Don't blame yourself, Ed. You were right. I wouldn't have figured he'd try again."

Ed turned and walked back to his horse. He had expected to have his hide ripped off, but Jeremy White had his mind on other things. Then, suddenly, Ed knew what that strange expression was. White was anticipating what was ahead, anticipating it and enjoying it just as a small boy would anticipate Christmas.

A chill raveled down Ed's spine. He thought, *My God, how can anybody feel that way? He's going to get somebody and it won't make any difference to him whether it's the right man or not.*

The last man rode in a moment later. White said, "We won't come back till we do what we're starting out to do. Tom Wheeler's in town keeping his eyes and ears open. I look for our man to go to town and make a show of himself, figuring that the town people are all so scared of Clegg they'll give him an alibi. If Tom has spotted him, we'll take him. If he hasn't, we'll go to Skull. If we still don't find him, we'll hang Sam Clegg himself. Any questions?"

Nobody said anything. "All right then," White said. "Mount up."

"I don't want to go," Tad said.

"You're going," White said in a low, tight voice.

Tad turned toward his horse, slipped his rifle into the boot, and mounted. For just a moment White stared at the boy, then he swung into the saddle and rode toward town, Tad beside him, the rest following.

Ed, riding behind Tad, wished he could do something for him, but he couldn't. You didn't buck Jeremy White, not if you wanted to live.

20

Sam Clegg ate breakfast with the crew by lamplight, then ordered them to saddle up. He returned to the house, buckled his gun belt around him, and picked up his Winchester. This was the first time in years that he had worn his gun. With men like Dutch Manders and Chick Lund to carry out his orders, he'd had no reason to pack a gun. Now Manders was dead.

He took his Stetson off the antler rack near the front door, clapped it on his head, and went on out into the pale morning light. His men were mounted, waiting. The chore boy had saddled his big, black gelding. He put a foot into the stirrup and swung up, then he remembered something.

"Louie, Larry Bain has a load of supplies that we need," Clegg said. "It should have come up from Cheyenne yesterday. You take a wagon and fetch it from town."

The chore boy nodded and stepped back. He was big and strong and not very bright, but he could be trusted to carry out a simple order like that. Clegg rode north, his men stringing out behind. Chick Lund and Bones Porter were next to him. Red Schone was the last in line.

Half an hour later Clegg reined up on the top of the ridge between the North and South Forks of the Slow Water. He turned his horse, his gaze running over his men. He said, "Chick, you'll head up the North Fork. You don't need any orders. You know what to do if you find Baron."

He named the men who would go with Lund, keeping Bones Porter in his bunch because he was remembering that if it hadn't been for Porter, Jim Baron would be dead and Dutch Manders would be alive and the whole damned world would look better. He kept Red Schone, too, largely because he wasn't sure Lund could keep the boy in line.

He looked at Lund. "Any questions, Chick?"

The cowboy grinned a little. "No. It's like you said, Boss. We'll know what to do when we find him."

"All right," Clegg said curtly. "Let's ride."

He wheeled his black and headed east along the ridge. No one said a word. They all knew that death for Jim Baron was the objective. They were six men going after one, a fact that went against the grain of some of them including Bones Porter. Others were like Red Schone. All they wanted was to see Baron swinging from a cottonwood limb, and that, Clegg told himself grimly, was exactly what he wanted.

They swung down off the ridge when they were directly above Ed Majors' place, forded the North Fork, and rode up to the buildings. A poverty outfit if Clegg had ever seen one. A small shack, a slab shed for a barn, a pole corral, a privy, and tiny slab shed and woven-wire pen for the chickens.

No grass, no flowers, a white spot in the front of the door where Majors had thrown his dishwater, and a stinking pile of tin cans and egg shells and potato peelings at one end of the shack. It was plain enough that no woman lived here.

"Red and Clinker look in the outbuildings," Clegg said. "Bones and Lee take the shack. Me'n Harry will cover you if anything breaks, which I don't figure will happen. Looks to me like Majors has pulled his freight."

The four men dismounted and searched the place. Harry Riis, the cowboy Clegg had ordered to stay with him, said, "Suppose they turn Ed Majors up?"

"That'd sure be too bad for Majors," Clegg said.

Not that he cared anything about Majors. Dead or alive, the man meant nothing to Sam Clegg, but he was Jim Baron's friend, and if he made any kind of a wrong move, he'd be a dead duck. If he didn't make a wrong move, well, the chances were he would.

A moment later the four men returned to the horses.

No one was around. Clegg glanced at the willows, wondering if Majors or Jim Baron had seen them coming and had taken refuge in the brush. There was one way to find out.

"Turn the stock loose," Clegg said, "then burn him out. Burn everything."

"Sam, wait a minute," Bones Porter said. "That ain't gonna make us nothing."

"Burn him out," Clegg said.

Schone and Lee and Clinker obeyed. Bones Porter stood motionless, staring at Clegg as if he were a stranger, and one he didn't like at that. Clegg didn't say a word. He told himself he'd pay Porter off and get rid of him the minute they got back to Skull. He wondered why he hadn't done it before.

Within a matter of minutes the buildings were in flames. There was no use to wait. If Jim and Majors were hiding in the brush, the fire would probably have brought them into the open. Clegg turned his back and rode upstream, the others following. Porter and Riis held back, but they, too, finally fell into line.

Damn Porter, Clegg thought angrily, Riis was a good man without Porter's disruptive influence, but Porter had been a good man up until he'd helped Chick Lund beat and kick Jim Baron. Since then he'd acted like an ornery, mossy horn bull that didn't want to go with the herd. Hard to figure a man like that.

When they reached the B-in-a-Box, Clegg saw that Jim's buckskin was not in the corral. They probably wouldn't find him, but they'd look and then they'd burn the buildings. That would bring Jim to Skull in a hurry if he managed to elude them today.

They reined up, Clegg saying, "Bones, stay with me. We'll cover. Harry and Clinker look in the house. Red and Lee take the outbuildings."

"No burning," Porter said.

The anger that had been smoldering in Clegg now soared. He demanded, "You starting to give the orders?"

"That was one I didn't want to hear you give," Porter snapped.

"By God, it looks like I'd better show you who's running the outfit," Clegg bellowed.

"There's a woman here," Porter said. "That makes a difference."

Clegg had forgotten all about Rose. Just then she came onto the porch, calling, "Come in, Mr. Clegg. I've got the coffeepot on the stove."

She made him sick. She was like her dad. Hank Baron always figured that if he bowed and scraped enough in front of you, you'd love him. Well, it just didn't work that way. The truth was Sam Clegg had far more respect for Jim Baron than he did his sister or had ever had for his father.

If Jim had known how to make a few concessions, Clegg would have welcomed him as a son-in-law, but Jim Baron was a man who couldn't give an inch. Neither could Clegg, so Jim had to be destroyed.

"Mr. Clegg, did you hear me?" Rose called.

"I don't have time," he answered in a surly voice. "Is Jim here?"

"No, he was supposed to be home last night," Rose said, "but he didn't come."

"Where is he?"

"I don't know," Rose said. "I guess he didn't get back from Cheyenne."

Red and Lee had finished searching the barn and turned toward one of the sheds. Riis and Clinker had stopped in front of Rose. She stood motionless, staring at Clegg as if she couldn't figure out what was happening. Now Clinker and Lee stepped up on the porch.

"What do you think you're doing?" Rose cried. "You get back off of here."

Clinker grinned. "Not till we've searched the house for Jim, then we figure to burn your buildings. It's time your brother learned he made a bad mistake when he tried bucking Skull."

She screamed an oath and struck at him like a cat, her

finger nails raking the side of his face and bringing blood. "Damn you," Clinker bawled, and hit her on the cheek with an open palm, rocking her head. "Behave yourself, or we'll string you up alongside your brother."

They went past her into the house. Clegg felt a faint stirring of conscience as he watched this. He had never hurt a woman physically in his life and Clinker was an animal for striking Rose. Still, she'd asked for it. Maybe he would have done the same if he'd been in Clinker's place.

Porter dismounted. Clegg asked, "What are you fixing to do, Bones?"

"I dunno," Porter said uneasily, "but I don't like the smell of this."

"You're fired," Clegg said. "You don't have the guts it takes to ride for Skull."

"You can't fire a man who's just quit," Porter said, "and that's what I done when you burned Majors out. That was stupid because there wasn't no reason for it. You made a big mistake there and I don't want a hand in this game any more."

Clegg didn't argue. Porter could think what he damned pleased. He was weak and Clegg had no room on Skull for a weak man. He saw Schone and Lee come out of one of the sheds, and then he was aware that Rose had run out of the house and was coming straight at him, a shotgun in her hands.

For the first time in his life Sam Clegg was paralyzed by fear, his stomach contracting so he couldn't breathe. She was going to kill him.

She started to raise the shotgun as she eased back the hammer. She'd blast a hole in him big enough to stick your fist in. He yelled, "No, no," and yanked his big black around and dug in the steel. He heard a shot and looked back, knowing it was not the shotgun that had been fired.

He saw Rose stumble and stagger three steps and then fall forward on her face. When she hit the ground, the shotgun went off, the buckshot flying harmlessly across the yard. Clegg pulled his horse down, still not knowing what had happened until he saw Red Schone standing in front of the shed, his smoking gun in his hand.

The next second another gun roared and Schone was knocked back against the wall of the shed. He hung there for a few seconds, bracing his legs and trying to bring his gun up into line, but he couldn't find the strength. Then his feet went out from under him and he went down.

Clegg could guess what had happened before he looked at Bones Porter. He saw Porter replace his gun; he saw Porter turn to him. For a moment he was strongly tempted to pull his own gun and smoke Porter down, but the damage had been done, so there was no point in doing that now. Besides, a warning nagged at the back of his brain. He didn't know how the other two would perform, Riis especially.

"You fool," Clegg said. "Couldn't you see he saved my life?"

"I'd have stopped her," Porter said. "I was reaching to knock the barrel of her shotgun down when he got her. It's murder and if I hadn't drilled him, we'd all be in trouble."

"The hell we would," Clegg snarled. "We're Skull. Lately you've forgotten that."

"Lately you've forgotten what Skull can and can't do," Porter said sharply. "Do you know what Schone done? He played right into Jeremy White's hands. It's the one thing Buck Riley can't overlook."

Clegg didn't say a word. He stared at Rose's gaunt body, lying there on her face in the dust of the yard, blood spreading across her back. Bones Porter was right. Killing a woman was one thing Skull could not do.

Clegg swung his black around, and rode away. He did not look until he topped the ridge, and then he saw that they had loaded Schone's body on his horse and were following. He turned his head, asking himself how these things could possibly be happening?

He had no answer.

21

Jim built a cook fire very early, the night chill that lingered in the canyon making the girls shiver as they cooked breakfast. He kicked out the fire as soon as they had eaten and sat down to wait. It seemed a long time before they heard horses far below them in the canyon.

Jim looked around the clearing to be sure he had not left anything in the open for the Skull men to see. He turned to the girls. "For the last time I'm asking you two to get on your horses and ride out of here. I can handle this business."

"Are you crazy?" Carrie asked indignantly. "I'm glad it's the last time you're going to ask us. Why do you think we came and where would we go? There's nothing up the canyon for us and if we went downstream we'd run right into them."

"I don't think you understand yet how I feel," Nora said. "If Sam's men found me here, they'd take me to Skull. Jim, I don't want to see Sam again. Not ever. Do you have any idea what it is to be kissed and hugged by him? I don't care if he is Carrie's father. To me he's just a nasty old man."

"I didn't pick him for a father," Carrie said, tight-lipped. "After while you get to the place where you don't claim him any longer. That's where I am."

"You didn't solve anything coming up here, Nora," Jim said.

"Maybe I didn't," she said glumly, "but I couldn't stay there."

Jim looked at Carrie and then at Nora, and he knew there was no use to argue with them. When it came to stubbornness, Carrie had a lot of Clegg in her. After they were married, they would meet problems in which he would do all the giving because she wouldn't.

"You're going to be hard to live with, Carrie," he said.

She gave him a straight look. "You still want to marry me?"

"I sure do." He couldn't help grinning at her. "All right, you're staying here, providing you'll do what I tell you."

"Of course we will," Nora said.

But Carrie wasn't so agreeable. "We aim to help you. We don't intend to sit back there in the brush and twiddle our thumbs while we stare at the sky."

"No, I ain't asking you to do that," he said. "I want you to hide yonder in the brush with your rifles and not show yourself and not even fire a shot unless you have to. I'm going to wade across the creek and hide on the other side."

He glanced downstream, pausing for a moment to listen, then he went on, "I'm guessing they'll ride in and smell the smoke and get down and feel of the ashes. About the time they decide I've gone on up the creek, I'll jump 'em. I'll tell 'em we've got 'em on both sides. If they don't believe me, fire a couple of shots just to show 'em you're there, but stay out of sight."

Carrie nodded. "We can do that. They'll be easier to handle if they think we're men."

"That's right." Jim cocked his head again to listen, then he said, "They're getting pretty close, so we'd better get set for 'em."

He waited until the girls were out of sight in the brush, then he circled the clearing to find out if he could see them from any part of it. Satisfied that both of them were well hidden, he waded the creek and hunkered behind a boulder to wait.

They rode into the clearing within five minutes, Chick Lund in front. They had their guns in their hands, not reining up until they reached the ashes of the cook fire. They looked around warily, then Lund holstered his gun and dismounted. Kneeling beside the ashes, he examined them. He rose, nodding.

"Baron ain't far ahead of us," Lund said. "We've got all day. We'd better rest our horses. The climb gets tougher about a mile above here. If he stays in the canyon, we'll bottle him up because there's a slide on up a piece that'll stop him."

The other five dismounted. One of them, a gangling man named Spider Webb, asked, "You figure six of us can handle him?"

Lund cursed. "You trying to crack a joke or something? I can handle him myself if we can find him."

They had gathered around the ashes, as tightly bunched as they would ever be. Jim stepped away from the boulder, his gun in his hand. "Hoist 'em," he said. "We've got you covered from both sides, so don't try to make a fight out of it. You'll be committing suicide if you do."

They wheeled to face him, surprised, then Lund laughed. "What kind of a sandy are you trying to run, Baron? You think we're stupid enough to believe you could find anyone to side you?"

A red-faced man named Rufe Smith edged away from the others, his right hand moving surreptitiously toward his gun. Jim hoped the girls saw what he was doing. Jim's gun covered Lund, and if he swung it from Lund to cut Smith down, Lund would draw. Jim couldn't possibly get his gun lined on Lund soon enough to get him.

Jim pretended he didn't see what Smith was doing. He nodded at Lund. "You walked right into it, Chick. Manders had some sense and Bones Porter is smart enough, but you don't have a brain in your head. I don't know why Sam keeps you around, let alone pay you fighting wages the way he does."

Smith's fingers were wrapped around the butt of his gun. He never drew it. Two rifles cracked from the north side of the clearing, one bullet lifted his hat off his head, the second kicked up a geyser of dust at his feet.

"That's purty good shooting, ain't it, Rufe?" Jim asked. "You're just about as smart as Chick. I could have plugged you right in the brisket. That would have given Chick a crack at me, but you would have been a dead duck. You making enough to afford that, Rufe?"

Smith's face was redder than ever. Lund began to curse, and now Jim was aware that he had stretched this out long enough. He said, "All right, we're done playing. Drop your gun belts and move away from the horses."

They obeyed, none of them wanting to argue now that they knew two rifles were covering them from the brush. "Fine, fine," Jim said. He waded back across the creek, nodding at Lund. "I heard you say while ago you could handle me, Chick. You handled me purty good the last time with Manders holding a gun on me and when there was three of you. This time you can try it yourself with no one holding me. If any of your tough hands jump into it, they're dead."

"You wouldn't give me a fair fight," Lund said. "Not with two rifles . . ."

Jim had already stripped off his gunbelt. He moved toward Lund, motioning to him. "Come on. You wouldn't know a fair fight if you saw one, but you'll get one anyhow."

Lund drove at him, both fists swinging. He got in one punch to the side of Jim's face and that was all. The fury and hatred and bitterness that had piled up in Jim from the day of his beating exploded. He drove a crashing right to Lund's chin that staggered him. Jim was on him immediately, giving him no chance to recover.

Lund caught a fist in the belly, one in the face again, and once more in the belly. All he could do was to back up and try to protect himself, but he couldn't hold Jim off any more than he could have held off an enraged bull. A sledging, turning fist flush to the jaw put him down. He staggered up, shook his head, and was promptly knocked down again.

This time Lund did not get up. He muttered, "I'm whipped, Baron." He wiped a hand across his battered mouth, and said again, "I'm whipped."

Jim heard an involuntary gasp from the Skull men, then he turned and walked back to his gun belt. Stooping, he picked it up and buckled it around him, then motioned to the five who were watching, eyes on Lund as if not believing this had really happened.

"Pull off your boots," Jim ordered.

"Now wait a minute," Rufe Smith shouted. "You ain't gonna make us . . ."

"I sure am," Jim drew his gun and cocked it. "Now get 'em off. If you'd got the drop on me, you'd have a rope on my neck before this. Can you think of any reason why I shouldn't smoke you down like a bunch of mangy, chicken-stealing coyotes?"

They didn't say a word. They tugged off their boots, then Jim said, "Now your pants." They looked at his face and obeyed without argument, and stood in their stocking feet, their shirttails flapping.

Suddenly Carrie began to laugh. She cried out, "Spider, I never knew how you got your nickname before, but now that I've seen you in your drawers, I know. You must have the longest and skinniest legs in the state of Wyoming."

"What the hell?" Webb muttered. "Is that Carrie?"

"You're right," Jim said. "One man and two women caught six Skull hard cases. When folks in Wheatridge hear about it, they'll know you ain't so damned hard, not any of you." He motioned to Lund who was still on the ground. "Get him on his horse. The rest of you are hoofing it out of here. When you get back to Skull pick up your belongings and keep going."

"We'll get you, Baron," Rufe Smith said. "By God, we'll hang you sure."

"I don't think so," Jim said. "I'd say that Skull was about finished. Even if it ain't, you boys are. All right, hoist him into the saddle."

He held his gun on them while they lifted the groaning, cursing Lund onto his horse. Then, with Smith leading the animal, they started downstream, Lund hanging to the horn as he swayed uncertainly from one side to the other.

Jim watched them until they were out of sight, walking gingerly over the rocky trail that followed the creek, then he motioned for the girls to come out of the brush.

"You're a hard man," Nora said.

He looked at her. "Three of 'em took me," he said. "I still hurt where they kicked me in the ribs. They came up here to kill me and you call me a hard man."

"I'm sorry," she said and looked away. "I'm not used to . . . to seeing things like that."

Carrie wasn't listening. She was staring downstream, her forehead tightened in a thoughtful frown. "Jim, I think you're right about Skull being finished. The reputation that Pa spent years building will be gone the minute those men show up in Wheatridge without their pants."

He turned to the horses, stripped gear from them, and drove them up the canyon. Eventually they would drift back to Skull, but not in time to do the five men who were on foot any good. Jim picked up the gun belts and tossed them across the creek into the willows.

"I'll build a fire and you women can cook dinner," he said. "I figure we might as well enjoy ourselves. I don't look for our friends to come back."

"No, they won't be back." She put her hands on her hips and smiled at him. "It strikes me that you've got a pretty good proposition with two squaws to boss around."

"It would be a good proposition," he agreed, "if one of the squaws didn't do most of the bossing."

He built the fire, then lay on his back in the grass beside the creek and stared at the sky. For the first time in days he felt relaxed and at peace as if he were on an island removed from the greed and hate and lust for power which flowed past him in a turbulent flood.

The peace, he thought with regret, would not last long. He had better enjoy it while he could.

22

Ed Majors had a hunch and he didn't like it. Jeremy White had not spelled out what they were going to do and nobody had asked him. None of the men talked about it on the way into Wheatridge. Ed guessed they were all like him. He didn't want to talk about it or even think about it, but the hunch stayed right there in the back of his mind. They were going to hang a man.

In spite of himself, Ed did think about it. He had liked Parson Bean. Everybody had. He had been a good and kindly man who had possessed very little in the way of material wealth, but he would have shared the little he did have with anyone who was more in need than he was.

His murder had been brutal and uncalled for and unnecessary. Buck Riley would fumble around and do nothing. A lynching was in order, Ed told himself. It was the only way the killer would be punished. Still, all of this self-assurance didn't really do the job. Ed couldn't entirely drive another thought out of his mind. *They might hang the wrong man.*

Jeremy White signaled for the column to stop before they reached the east end of Main Street. He said, "Tad, go in and find Tom Wheeler. Fetch him back here."

The boy nodded and rode on into town. White stepped out of his saddle and walked back and forth across the road. Some of the others dismounted and stretched. No one said a word. Ed decided they were all thinking the same thing he was. He knew what was coming with a certainty that he had never felt about any future event in his life before, and he wasn't going to say a word or raise a hand to stop it.

Rudy Simms, one of White's hired men, walked up to him and said something. White nodded and said, "Three of us can do it."

Simms remained beside White until Tad and Tom Wheeler rode up five minutes later. White stood with one hand on the butt of his gun, his head tipped back, questioning eyes on Wheeler.

"He's there," Wheeler said. "Calls hisself Pete Hammer, but he's Ham Peterson, all right. Came up on the stage from Cheyenne with Tad and Mrs. White and Jim Baron. Talking big like always. Says he heard there was a range war beginning to pop and he figured he might just as well have some of that big money for hisself."

"When did he ride into town?"

"I dunno," Wheeler said. "Maybe half an hour ago. I was standing in front of the Palace when they opened up and he wasn't there then. Fact is, I didn't see him ride up, but he came into the saloon 'bout half an hour ago."

"That'd give him plenty of time," White said. "He shot the Parson and rode away from there. Chances are he circled town and came in from the west so it'd look like he'd been at Skull all the time." White scratched his chin. "Did he see you? I mean, did he recognize you?"

"I don't think so," Wheeler said. "I was playing solitaire at a corner table and I kept my head down. He went right to the bar and had a drink. He started blowing off first thing to the bartender and a couple of businessmen who had dropped in for an eye opener."

White nodded. "Carstairs wasn't around?"

"I didn't see him," Wheeler answered, "but there was another fellow who got off the stage last night with our man Hammer. I was at the other end of the block, but he was built like Carstairs. I'll bet that was him, but I wasn't sure like I was of this Hammer."

"If it's our old friend Ham Peterson, or Hammer as he calls himself now," White said, "Carstairs is bound to be around here somewhere." White turned to the men behind him. "The killer's in the Palace. We're going to take him. Rudy, Tom and me will go into the Palace after him. You men stay outside and keep Buck Riley off our backs. Or any Skull hands who are in town. Savvy?"

The men nodded, all but Ed who still didn't like what

was coming, but still didn't intend to stop it. That strange, almost obscene expression was on White's face. He would have shot down in cold blood any man who tried to stop him. Ed didn't intend to be that man.

"All right, cover your faces," White ordered.

He pulled his flour sack from his pocket, slipped it over his head, and glanced behind him. When he saw that all of them were masked, he said, "We'll go in fast, get it over with fast, and get out of town fast. Let's ride."

White led out at a gallop, Tad keeping up beside him, Simms and Wheeler behind him, the rest of the column strung out without any plan or order. Chickens, dogs, and children scattered before them as they thundered into town. They reined up before the Palace, White the first out of the saddle. He went through the batwings on the run, his gun in his hand. Simms and Wheeler were a step or two behind him.

Ed, his rifle held across his saddle, looked around. He saw only two horses tied anywhere on the street, one here in front of the Palace. Neither was a Skull horse, but the one tied at the Palace hitch rack was a livery stable animal, so it was probably the horse that Pete Hammer, or Ham Peterson, had rented. The few people who had been on the street had disappeared. Buck Riley was not in sight, but Ed hadn't expected him to be.

He heard White say in a cold, biting tone, "We're taking Hammer for the murder of Parson Bean. The rest of you stay out of it and you won't get hurt. Bartender, send word to Clegg that he'll be the next if another settler is murdered."

A moment later Wheeler and Simms came out of the saloon, dragging a man between them. He was cursing and shouting that he was innocent. He hadn't murdered anybody. He'd stayed all night at Skull, he'd ridden into town for breakfast, and he'd been here ever since. He couldn't have murdered anybody.

No one paid any attention to him. Wheeler and Simms hoisted him into his own saddle. Ed guessed it was his, and apparently Wheeler and Simms thought so, too.

Simms tied his hands behind his back, mounted, and, taking the reins, led the horse toward the courthouse. Wheeler followed, the rest except White riding behind.

Jeremy White had been the last one out of the saloon, backing through the batwings and keeping his gun on the men inside the saloon. Now he ran to his horse, mounted, and raced on ahead to the courthouse. By the time Simms arrived with Pete Hammer, White had shaken his rope out and tossed one end over a limb.

Hammer was crying like a child. He kept whimpering, "I didn't do it. I tell you I didn't do it."

Ed had told himself over and over he wasn't going to say a word or do anything to stop it, but now he heard himself asking, "Jerry, how do you know this man done it?"

"He's the one, all right," White said without as much as a glance at Ed. He had dropped the loop over Hammer's head and tightened it around his throat. Wheeler had tied the other end to a nearby tree. Now White said, "Stand up on your saddle."

"I can't," Hammer said. "I can't."

White stepped back and drew his gun. "Then I'll shoot you right there."

I'd make him do it if it was me, Ed told himself.

Hammer must have thought they were only trying to scare him. Somehow he managed to get his feet out of the stirrups and up on the saddle. He heaved himself upright and swayed back and forth. Tears ran down his face as he alternately begged for his life and cursed a man he called Keno Ross, nobody Ed had ever heard of.

"Slap his horse with your hat," White said to Tad.

The boy shrank back. His face was covered the same as the others, but Ed guessed how he felt. He yelled at White, "I'll do it."

"No," White snarled. "The boy will. Tad, give the horse a cut."

The boy snatched off his hat and clouted the horse across the rump. Startled, the horse leaped forward, Hammer's body dropped and the rope snapped tight. His neck must have been broken at once. He swung back and forth like a giant pendulum, his head cocked grotesquely to one side, his tongue protruding from his mouth. White drew his gun, pronged back the hammer, and shot him in the chest. Quickly he mounted, dug in the steel, and rocketed out of town, the rest following.

Tad was swaying in his saddle. Ed rode close to him, afraid he would faint, and all the time he kept asking himself what kind of man was Jeremy White who would bring his son to a lynching party in the first place, and then force him to commit the actual act of killing the victim.

There seemed to be no sense to it, but Ed did know now there had been something between Jeremy White and his two men on one side, and this fellow Pete Hammer on the other along with someone named Carstairs who might, as Tom Wheeler believed, be the second man who had come in on the stage with Mrs. White and Tad. Ed wondered, too, if this feud, whatever it was, had more to do with the lynching than the murder of Parson Bean.

Ed still didn't think there was any evidence connecting Hammer and the Parson's murder. Regardless of Hammer's guilt or innocence, Ed Majors and the rest of the settlers were involved and were partly guilty of Hammer's lynching if Buck Riley or any other law officer wanted to pursue it. But all of this had nothing to do with Tad. The more he thought about it, the less sense there was for White making the boy do what he had.

They removed their masks when they were out of town and slowed their horses. No one was pursuing them and no one was likely to. Clegg and some of the Skull crew might come later, although Ed doubted it.

Tad had been crying. Ed watched the boy closely for a time, and when he felt sure he would be all right, he turned off the road and angled across the top of the ridge toward his place. Jeremy White had struck hard and brutally, and Ed wondered what Sam Clegg would think when he heard about Hammer's lynching. He might not be as tough and ambitious as he's thought, now that he'd found out what he was up against.

Then Ed reached the crest of the ridge and looked down at his place. He reined up, his breath going out of him with an audible sound. *He had been burned out.*

He couldn't believe it. He hadn't had much to lose and he'd intended to ride off in a day or two and leave what he did have, but still, to be burned out this way was more than he was going to take. It had to be Clegg or some of his men. After the first shock wore off, Ed realized he would have been killed if he had been home.

No reason to ride down there. He turned his horse and, following the edge of the ridge, rode east until it petered out. A few minutes later he reached the White place. Wheeler and Simms were hunkered down at the corral gate, smoking and whittling. Ed asked where Tad was, but neither knew. Then he asked for Jeremy and they nodded toward the house.

Ed rode to the front door and dismounted. White appeared on the porch, looking like a different man. He was tired, there were deep lines in his face, and his shoulders sagged.

"Clegg burned me out," Ed said. "Nothing's left and I'm broke."

"Put your horse up," White said. "Sleep in the bunkhouse tonight. Stay here till this is over. We can't think straight until it is."

"Thanks." Ed hesitated, then he asked, "We going after Clegg for burning me out?"

White shook his head. "We'll wait. It's his move now."

Ed started to turn away, then swung back. "Why would he burn my buildings? He's got no reason to be after me."

"Why did they murder Parson Bean?" White asked. "Why did Sam Clegg start this in the first place? You never answer questions like that, Ed. The only thing you can do is to hit a man like Clegg harder than he hits you. It's the only thing he ever understands."

White hesitated, staring across the valley, then he

added, "Maybe we'll have to burn him out. I don't guess even that would help, though. We won't have any peace until we kill him and before we're done, that's what we'll do."

Ed led his horse across the yard, stripped gear from him, and turned him into the corral. Then he squatted beside Wheeler and rolled a smoke. He said, "I'm burned out. Jerry said to stay here till the fight's over."

Both men nodded and went on whittling. Ed asked, "What happened between Jerry and this Pete Hammer, or Ham Peterson I guess he used to be?"

Wheeler nodded. "That's the name he used to go by."

Neither man said anything else for a time. Ed had not really expected an answer. In fact, he'd thought they'd curry his hide for even asking the question.

After a long silence Simms said, "Ain't no secret about it, I reckon. Not now that that bastard Peterson showed up on this range. Chances are Carstairs is here, too. Well, me'n Tom were with Jerry when he called himself Keno Ross. Hammer and Carstairs were on the other side of a Texas range war that dragged on for years. Finally Hammer and Carstairs rigged some evidence that made it look like Jerry had murdered the sheriff, so we had to vamoose."

"Funny you'd all get together on this range," Ed said. "We're a long ways from Texas."

"Not so funny," Wheeler said. "Hammer and Carstairs are drygulchers. They ain't gunfighters. When the word got out that Clegg and his bunch were in the market for a killer, Hammer and Carstairs came on the run."

"If Carstairs is around, we'll still get drygulched maybe," Ed said.

Wheeler nodded. "We'll get him. We've got to if we're gonna keep breathing."

Ed knew, then, why Jeremy White had looked so different on the porch just now. His life was in danger as long as Carstairs was alive and in the country, the same danger that had cut Parson Bean down.

23

The rest of the day was a nightmare for Sam Clegg. When he reached Skull, the chore boy, Louie, was gone, so Clegg had to take care of his horse himself. About half-way back the men who had been following him turned toward town. He supposed that Bones Porter wanted to tell Buck Riley what had happened.

When he went into the house, he yelled at Mrs. Horn that he was back. She didn't answer. He walked on to the kitchen and found a note on the table. "Keep the month's wages you offered me. You couldn't pay me enough to stay here."

He crumpled the note and threw it into the stove. He felt the same way. To hell with her. She was worse than nothing and he was glad to get rid of her. Tomorrow he would ride to town and see Nora. They might just as well get married now. She'd be pleased that he had made a new will leaving everything to her.

Carrie deserved nothing except the single dollar that he would leave her. Even that was too much. Later, if there were children, he'd change the will, but for the present, everything he owned would go to Nora when he died. Judge Carr hadn't approved, but Clegg didn't care about that. It was the way he wanted it.

He paced around the front room. He felt like a trapped wild animal. Nothing to do now but wait. Maybe Buck Riley would overlook Rose's killing and call it an accident. Or say that there was nothing to do now that Red Schone was dead. Even if Riley did come out to Skull, there wasn't anything he could do. Red Schone had fired the shot, not Sam Clegg, and you couldn't very well hang a dead man.

As far as Rose's killing was concerned, he couldn't be held responsible for what Schone had done. Still, he couldn't rid himself of the mental picture of Rose lying in the dust like a rag doll that had been carelessly tossed away by its owner. He kept telling himself she had tried to kill him. All he could do was to ask himself why, but there was only the question, never the answer.

Suddenly Clegg remembered about Hammer and Dillon and wondered if they were still in bed. He went upstairs and checked. Their rooms were empty. Hammer's warbag was on the floor beside his bed, but the rifle was gone.

Clegg went back downstairs to the living room and lighted a cigar. He sat down in his leather chair and tried to relax, but he couldn't. The clock struck twelve. He decided he'd rather rustle something to eat than to go to the cook shack and ask the cook to fix something. He threw his half-smoked cigar away and went to the door. Bones Porter and the men who had been with him should have showed up by now. He'd feel better if Chick Lund and the others who had gone after Jim Baron would ride in and tell him they had settled once and for all with Baron.

Clegg told himself he wasn't scared. He kept his gun belt buckled around his waist. There was just a chance that Jim Baron would show up out here and want to settle their differences personally. He assured himself he would welcome it. After he shot Baron, he'd take his crew as soon as they ate dinner, or supper if they rode in late, and they'd go down the Slow Water and wind up his fight with the settlers.

Then, suddenly, he remembered that Jim Baron had smoked Dutch Manders down, and he was shocked at how much he had underestimated Baron who was in no way like his father. He also remembered that Jeremy White was one of the settlers and he had misjudged White, too.

He stood in the doorway, sweat popping through the skin of his face. *He was alone.*

The full significance of this got through to him at last. He saw no one coming toward Skull from town, no one was coming over the ridge from the North Fork the way Chick Lund and his men would come.

There had been a day when Sam Clegg had been the best man with his fist in Slow Water County and he had proved it repeatedly. He'd had the fastest gun in the county, too, but he'd hired his fighting done too long, he'd depended on men like Dutch Manders and Chick Lund too long.

Manders was dead. Red Schone was dead. Maybe Lund had walked out on him. Bones Porter was no good to him any more. Well, there were plenty of men who had guns for hire, plenty of cowhands who needed work.

Sam Clegg had money, and when you have money, you can always hire men to do the things you need to have done. To hell with Lund and Porter and the rest of them. With that thought confidence returned to him and he went into the kitchen, found what was left of a roast and made a sandwich. He'd get along until suppertime when the men returned. He'd eat with them.

Just as he finished eating, he heard a wagon and, running out of the house, saw that it was Louie returning with the load of supplies. He waited until Louie reached him and pulled up, then he said in the bullying tone he used with the boy, "Took you a long time to go to town and get back."

Louie nodded and moistened his lips with the tip of his tongue. He said, "Something happened this morning, Boss. That bunch of White Caps, everybody says it's the settlers, rode into town and lynched that fellow Hammer who came out here last night."

Clegg stared at Louie. He didn't believe it. He said, "You're lying, Louie. That bunch of sodbusters wouldn't have the guts to do a thing like that."

"They done it and I ain't lying," Louie said. "I was back of Bain's store loading up when it happened. I didn't know anything about it till it was over with, and then I seen Hammer hanging from a limb of that big cottonwood in front of the courthouse. I watched 'em cut him down."

"Where was Buck Riley?"

Louie shrugged. "I dunno. I seen him help cut Hammer down, but I reckon he wasn't around when they was hanging him."

"Why? What had Hammer done?"

"I heard Larry Bain say he was in the Palace when they came in and got Hammer. He said they claim Hammer murdered Parson Bean."

"Bean?" The name was jolted out of Clegg. "Why would Hammer have murdered him?"

He almost said he'd told Hammer to start with Ed Majors, but he caught himself in time. It would take an idiot to kill Bean who was the best-liked man of any of the settlers and who had never done a thing to hurt anyone. He was the last man on the river to eliminate.

Louie sat on the wagon seat shaking his head. "I dunno, Boss. I sure dunno."

"You take the load around to the cook shack and unhook the team," Clegg said. "Then you saddle a horse and ride to the Rafter A and tell Ace Alred to get the other members of the Association and have them and their crews here by six tonight. If Riley can't arrest the lynchers, we'll take care of them ourselves."

Louie moistened his lips again, hesitated, and then said, "All right."

He drove away and Clegg went into the house. His men would be back before six, and with the other outfits, they could hit every settler's farm at the same time and wipe them out. It didn't make any difference how tough Jeremy White was. Clegg would have so many men he'd clean that batch of settlers out in a matter of minutes.

It seemed to Clegg that it took an eternity for Louie to saddle up and get started. After that the afernoon dragged. He tried to catch up on his book work, but he couldn't seem to add or even keep his mind on his business.

He opened his safe and counted the cash. There were two envelopes, one with $1500 which was his and Ace Alred's contribution to the fund that was to pay Pete

Hammer, but now Hammer was dead, so he'd give Alred's $500 back. He moved the $1000 which belonged to him to the other envelope which held his petty cash, enough to meet any sudden demands like paying off a hand he had fired. This envelope contained something over $1800 which was more than he liked to keep out here, but it was too late now to take it to town today to bank it.

This whole idea of hiring a drygulcher had been a bad one. He wondered now why he had ever listened when Alred had proposed it. The plan had sounded fine, but it hadn't worked out, mostly because Pete Hammer had been stupid, shooting off his mouth about working for Sam Clegg and then going out and drygulching the wrong man.

Clegg's way had always been the direct one, to simply run over anyone who stood in his way. If he had held to that principle and insisted that the Cattlemen's Association operate the same way, the whole business would have been over before now and the settlers would have been off the river. Alred had always been a sly one who liked to go at things in a roundabout way and for once Clegg had made the mistake of listening.

He went outside and prowled around the corrals and barns and all the time he wondered why Bones Porter and the men with him didn't return. Chick Lund, too. It was getting along toward six and he needed them when Alred and the other members of the Association rode in.

He returned to the house and a few minutes later saw four riders appear on the road from town. He watched until they were close enough to recognize. Porter and Clinker rode in front, Lee and Harry behind them.

Clegg took a long breath, feeling a great sense of relief. He guessed he wouldn't fire Porter after all. If he wanted to quit, well, that was his choice. At least the other three were back and he could depend on them.

They rode past the house to the bunkhouse and dismounted and went in, leaving their saddled horses in front. He hesitated, then decided he'd better tell them what the program was. They'd want fresh mounts, so they had better pull their saddles off these animals. He'd tell the cook to hurry supper up because time was short.

He strode to the bunkhouse, feeling better now that the men were back. He went inside and started to tell them that they were raiding the settlers in about an hour, then stopped, surprised and shocked and not knowing quite what to make of it. All four men were stowing their possessions into their warbags.

Porter straightened and looked at him. He said, "Sam, the news is all bad as far as you're concerned. We came back to get our stuff. We want to be paid. We're quitting."

"You can't do that," Clegg shouted. "I'll double your wages."

Porter actually looked sorry for him. He said, "I've worked for you for a long time. I don't know why I stayed as long as I did because it was damned plain what direction you were heading. We're done. All the money you've got ain't enough to hold us." He turned away. "Anyhow, you fired me."

"But . . . but . . ."

"I'll tell you something else," Clinker said. "On our way out here we ran into Chick and his outfit. They was on foot without their boots or their pants. Their feet were cut to pieces. They sure were a sorry-looking bunch. Chick was on his horse, but he looked like it was all he could do to stay in the saddle."

Porter straightened again and looked at Clegg. "That Jim Baron is quite a man, Sam. He took 'em when they reached the clearing where we gave him a beating and he gave Chick the same treatment. I'm glad I wasn't with 'em. Chick looked like he'd be in bed for a while."

Porter swung around and continued packing. Clinker said, "We want our time before we ride out."

Clegg walked through the door and back to the house. He moved automatically, putting one foot ahead of the other as if he were a stick figure. He went to his office, counted out the money for the four men, and returned to the bunkhouse. He gave each cowboy what he owed him and swung around and walked out without saying a word to them.

He dropped into his leather chair. He looked at the clock. Almost six. Alred and the others would be along any time now. He simply could not grasp what had happened today. It was impossible for the whole world to go sour the way it had in a matter of hours; it was not possible for one man, Jim Baron, to take the boots and pants and horses away from six men, six damned tough men who had been sent to get him and kill him.

No, it hadn't happened. It was just a story that Porter and Clinker and the others had made up and thought he'd be sucker enough to believe. Chick and his boys would be riding in any minute now.

But they didn't come. The clock struck six. He saw Porter and the other three ride past the house and take the road to town. Presently the clock struck seven and then eight, and the twilight gave way to darkness, but Ace Alred and the rest of his neighbors failed to appear.

Sam Clegg sat alone in the darkness, listening for the sound of hoofs that never came.

24

Edna White did not return home until it was time to get supper. When she stopped the buggy in front of the corral gate, Tom Wheeler walked to her and said he would take care of the mare. She saw Jeremy standing with Simms and Ed Majors beside the mowing machine. They were talking about something, but she couldn't hear what they were saying.

"Where's Tad?" she asked.

"I dunno," Wheeler mumbled. "I ain't seen him for quite a spell."

She didn't think any more about it at the time, but went into the house and started a fire in the range. Later, when she rang the supper gong, she saw that Ed Majors was still here, so she put an extra plate on the table when she went back into the kitchen.

Suddenly she remembered that she hadn't seen Tad. Usually he made an appearance when she was getting supper to try to scrounge something to eat. He always wanted to lick the icing bowl if she made a cake, and he'd steal a spoonful of dough if she didn't watch him.

She's needed an armload of wood and finally had gone out and brought it in herself. Now, when Jeremy came in with the other men, she asked, "Where is Tad? I haven't seen him since I got home."

The four men sat down at the table, Simms and Wheeler carefully avoiding looking at her. Ed Majors started to answer, then decided not to. Jeremy said casually as he reached for the meat platter, "I haven't seen him, Edna. Maybe he went hunting along the river and forgot to come home."

She shook her head, knowing that wasn't like him. It occurred to her he might be sick and had gone to bed.

She went into his room, and there he was, sprawled out on the bed, his eyes wide open.

She sat down on the edge of the bed. "I rang the supper bell. Didn't you hear?"

"I heard."

He didn't look at her. He kept staring at the ceiling and suddenly she had a strange feeling. She reached out and took his hand. It was cold, almost clammy, and she jerked her hand away and wiped her face with her handkerchief. She was terrified. For just an instant she had seen him laid out in a coffin.

"What is it, Tad?" she whispered.

"Nothing," he answered. "I just don't feel very good."

For a moment she sat there, staring at his pale, drawn face. She had always been close to him, much closer than Jeremy, and yet for some reason which had always eluded her, Tad respected and loved his father.

"Won't you come and eat your supper?" she asked.

"I'm not hungry," he said.

She rose. "I'll eat my supper and clean up the dishes. Then I'll come back."

He didn't say anything; he didn't even look at her. She left the room, going back into the kitchen just as the men were finishing and getting up from the table. "Something's happened to Tad," she said. "He's in his room, but he won't come out and eat."

Wheeler and Simms left the kitchen quickly. Ed Majors paused and looked at her thoughtfully, then he followed the other two. Jeremy said, "I guess he's upset over Parson Bean's murder. When's the funeral?"

"Tomorrow afternoon."

Jeremy went out then. She sat down at the table and tried to eat, but the food stuck in her throat. Finally she rose and cleaned up the table and washed and dried the dishes. By the time she finished, it was dark and she had lighted a lamp. Now she picked up the lamp and went into Tad's room. Apparently he hadn't moved.

"Sure you can't eat?"

"No. I'm not hungry."

"Tad, something happened. I want to know what it was."

He didn't answer for a long time. Finally, without looking at her, he said, "I killed the man who murdered the Parson. I guess he deserved it, all right, and if we hadn't hung him, nobody would have touched him. Buck Riley would have looked the other way like he always does, but I didn't want to do it. Now I keep seeing him with his mouth open and his tongue sticking out and his face turning black."

She sat there, frozen, hardly breathing. Finally she whispered, "Tell me about it."

He did, slowly and haltingly. He hadn't wanted to go with the White Caps in the first place, he said, and he hadn't wanted to slap the horse with his hat when it was time to hang the killer, but both times his father had made him do it.

When Tad finished talking, she remained in silence on the edge of the bed. Shocked, she thought of how Jeremy was really two men in one. Usually she had seen the kind and thoughtful one, but this thing he had done to Tad was the other one, the cold and distant man who enjoyed killing and must have enjoyed making his son kill.

A loaded Winchester hung from pegs beside the front door. Now she could see Jeremy laid out in a coffin just as she had seen Tad a while ago. She would kill Jeremy. He deserved killing for what he had done to her boy.

She rose finally. "Time will make you forget what you did," she said. "It wasn't your fault, so don't blame yourself. Your father made you do it."

Tad turned his head. His dark eyes seemed to be buried deep in his head. He licked his dry, cracked lips. "I wanted him to be proud of me," he said. "I guess I've never been a boy he could respect. I'm sorry because I'm proud of him. I wanted him to be proud of me."

Proud, she thought. *Proud of a father who was a gunman, a killer!*

She turned away, ashamed of herself because she had stayed with Jeremy all these years, ashamed of Tad because he loved his father so much and wanted to be loved by him. She said, "Why don't you try to sleep? In the morning we'll go away."

"No, I'm staying," he said. "You can go away if you want to, but I'm staying. Someday I will be the kind of man he's proud of. You'll see."

She left the boy's room, walking quickly and shutting the door behind her. She didn't want him to see her cry and she knew that was what she was going to do. It was enough to make any woman cry, to hear her son say he wanted to be the kind of man in whom Jeremy White would feel pride.

But she didn't cry. She stood with her back to the door for a good five minutes, her head bowed. The tears just wouldn't come. Maybe they were frozen. She felt that cold inside.

She moved slowly along the hall to hers and Jeremy's bedroom and went in. He was sitting on the edge of the bed tugging his boots off, his gun belt hanging over the back of a chair. He looked up, asking, "Where have you been? It's bedtime."

"I've been talking to Tad," she said.

He picked up his boots and set them against the wall. He was always neat, she thought, neat and precise and dead sure of himself in everything he did.

"He told you?" Jeremy asked.

"He told me."

"All right, now you know," he said. "Come to bed. I expect to finish this business tomorrow."

She didn't move. She stood staring down at him, hating him and wondering if she could actually kill him. Finally she said, "I'll never lie in the same bed with you again. You're not a man. You're some kind of a monster to do what you did to a boy like Tad."

He smiled, the cold, impersonal smile she had seen on his face a few times. "I'm not surprised, hearing you say that. I've left him alone too much, particularly too much with you. You're trying to make some kind of a hothouse plant out of him. Well, I won't stand for it. I promise you I'll make a man out of him."

"I'm going to town to live in the morning," she said. "I'm taking Tad with me."

He unbuttoned his shirt and took it off. "You're free to go if you want to," he said indifferently, "but you won't take Tad. I doubt that he would go with you anyhow."

She started to turn away from him, then paused as he went on, "Edna, I guess you never understood why I came here. I told you no one would think of looking for me here. That was one reason and it was a good one, but there was another better reason. When we were in Texas I had to leave Tad with you far too much. I saw what you were doing to him, so when I had to leave, I came here with a notion that someday I'd have a cattle ranch and I'd build it for Tad.

"I was damned tired of doing the dirty work for other cattle kings. I figure I might just as well be one myself and Tad would help build the outfit. Right now we've got to fight for it, but in time we'll have a spread like Skull or Alred's Rafter A. While I'm building our outfit, I'll make a man out of Tad. You can stay and help, or walk out. It's up to you."

She went on into the living room. A moment later he blew the lamp out. She stood in the doorway for a time, looking into the darkness, then she stepped outside and sat on the porch and stared at the black sky with its sharp and brilliant stars. The tears were very close again.

The feeling in her was strong that she faced a complete change. She wasn't sure what the future held, but at least she was sure that this was the end of her way of life. Perhaps Tad wouldn't go with her. If he didn't, she'd stay in Wheatridge just to be close to him if he needed her. He would. She knew he would.

Somehow she wore the night out, sitting on the porch or lying down on the couch in the front room. She didn't sleep. The coldness still lay deep inside her and she wondered if it would ever go away. When it was dawn, she returned to the porch and sat there again and watched the eastern sky turn red and the light slowly deepen.

She heard someone cross the front room. Looking around, she saw that it was Tad.

"Are you hungry yet?" she asked. "I'll start breakfast if you are."

"No, I'm not hungry," he said. "I just couldn't stay inside any longer."

She hesitated, then she said, "Honey, I'm going to town to live. I'm leaving your father. Will you go with me?"

"No," he said. "I told you."

She sighed, knowing she could not beg him. If this was his decision, he would have to live with it and there was nothing more she could do for him.

"All right," she said. "I'm going to pack up now. Would you harness the mare for me? I'll take the buggy and you can go with me and bring it back."

He nodded as he stepped off the porch and walked on across the yard toward the barn. He was halfway there when the rifle shot cracked from the willows. She saw Tad stagger and go down. She screamed. She wasn't aware she was screaming until she heard the sound of her voice. She was on her feet and running toward him, not even thinking that the assassin might shoot her, too.

She knelt beside Tad and lifted his head to her lap. He was dead. The bullet had struck him in the chest and now blood spread across his shirt front and bubbled at the corners of his mouth. The feeling hit her that this was familiar. She had known that something like this would happen. It was almost as though she had lived through this terrible moment before.

Jeremy was there, then, still buttoning his pants. Wheeler and Simms ran out of the bunkhouse, Ed Majors a step behind them, buckling his gun around his waist as he strode toward them. Jeremy said, "It was Carstairs. It had to be. Tad's about my height. He thought Tad was me!"

She eased Tad's head off her lap and stood up. She looked at Jeremy and knew without the slightest doubt that she could kill him. He hadn't pulled the trigger, but he had killed Tad just the same. If he hadn't taken Tad with the White Caps yesterday and made him whip the horse out from under the man they were hanging, Tad would not have left the house at this hour. Usually he didn't get out of bed until she had called him three or four times.

She whirled and walked back into the house. She took the Winchester off the pegs and levered a shell into the chamber. She left the house and walked swiftly across the yard.

Jeremy's back was to her. He was saying, "Saddle up. The four of us are enough. He'll go back to Skull to collect from Clegg, figuring he had beefed me. We'll get both of them."

She was only two steps from him when she stopped. She said, "Jeremy."

He wheeled, asking impatiently, "What do you want?"

She shot him three times. He was dead before he fell.

Dropping the rifle, she turned to Ed Majors. "Ed, will you harness the team and hook them up to the wagon. I'll pack what I need and I'll surrender to the sheriff. Wrap Tad's body in a blanket and put it in the wagon. We'll bury him in town."

She walked to the house, not looking back.

25

When the sun rose Sam Clegg was still in his leather chair. He had slept a few minutes at a time, then he would wake up and tell himself there was no sense staying up this way, that if Ace Alred and the other Association members intended to come, but had been delayed for some reason, they would have sent word before now.

That was the logic of it, and Clegg had always been a very logical man. Too, he had been a man of action who controlled events, never permitting events to control him. Now he was not being logical, and he had no compulsion as he would normally have had to get up and saddle his horse and ride to the Rafter A to see what was holding Alred up.

Later, when daylight finally drove the last of the night shadows from the room, he rose and, going to the sideboard, poured a stiff drink of whiskey and returned to his chair. The whiskey did not change anything.

For now, he told himself, he would wait. An hour passed, then two, and the room became warm. Presently he heard a rider outside. Chick Lund, he thought. Or Alred. No, if it were either man, he would not be alone. Jim Baron? An involuntary prickle ran down his spine. Surely not Baron. The screen opened and slammed shut; he heard the jingle of spurs and a man said, "Clegg."

The fingers of his right hand were wrapped around the butt of his gun, but if this was Jim Baron, he would never get the revolver out of leather in time to defend himself. Baron would shoot him to death right here in his chair. He was surprised to discover that he didn't really care.

Slowly he forced himself to turn his head to see who had come in. The man stood a little behind him and to one side. Breath came out of Clegg in a gusty sigh. It was R. C. Dillon.

"You find some land to develop?" Clegg asked shakily.

Dillon laughed. It was not a good laugh. Clegg sensed there was no humor in it, there was no humor in the man's eyes, either. He still had the dead-fish expression that Clegg had seen there before.

"I don't know whether you're joshing me or if you're a fool," Dillon said, "but most of the cowmen I've worked for have been fools and I reckon you're no different. I came for my two thousand dollars, then I'm getting to hell out of this country before I get what they gave Pete Hammer."

Clegg rubbed his face with both hands. This had to be a nightmare. Dillon didn't make any sense. What had he done to earn $2000? He asked, "You heard about Hammer?"

"Yeah, I heard," Dillon said. "It was the first real mistake we ever made and we'd been working together for years. I'm the one who made it. I should have known better because I knew Keno Ross . . . Jeremy White, I mean . . . was tough." He shook his head. "Neither one of us figured he could turn a bunch of homesteaders into a band of White Caps that would have the guts to hang either one of us."

Clegg stared at Dillon, wondering if it was the whiskey, or if it really was a nightmare so real he thought this was actually happening. Or was he as loco as he was afraid he was?

"I just don't savvy, Dillon," he said finally. "I didn't know you and Hammer were working together. All I know is that he was a bigger fool than he had any right to be. I told him to get Ed Majors, but instead he shot Parson Bean. It was Bean's murder that turned them farmers into a lynch mob. Everybody liked him, even people who weren't settlers."

Dillon gave him a look of sheer contempt. He made an impatient gesture, saying sharply, "Get up out of that chair and go get my money. Damn it, I haven't got all day. If I don't turn this horse in before I leave the country or buy it from the livery stable, the law will be on my tail for horse stealing and I can't afford that. I want to get paid for carrying out my end of the contract, so quit stalling."

Still Clegg sat there, staring at Dillon. He said, "I sure don't know what you've done to earn any money. If you and Hammer had been working together, I should think you'd be a little sorry for what happened . . ."

"Oh, I am. I'm sorry because now I've got to find a new partner or start operating differently than I have been." Dillon stopped, his eyes narrowing, then he said, "Maybe you ain't stalling. Maybe you are just as stupid as you act. All right, I'll explain it in simple words so you'll savvy, then maybe you'll get my dinero. Pete was the one who made the big noise when we showed up on a range to fulfill a contract. People heard him talk and saw him and figured he was the one who pulled the trigger when a man turned up dead, but he always had an alibi so the law never could touch him and I was always gone before anybody thought of me. The trouble this time was that the lynch mob never waited to hear his alibi."

"Then you're the one who shot Parson Bean," Clegg asked. "Why? I told Hammer to get Ed Majors."

"Sure, sure," Dillon said impatiently. "He told me what you said after you went to bed and gave me the map. I tried for Majors and missed for the first time in my life. I should have waited a few more minutes until the light was better, but I thought I could get both Majors and White and we could leave the country. After I missed Majors, I figured you just wanted two men rubbed out, so I rode down the creek and got Bean. By that time it was too late to go after White, so I pulled out. I got him this morning, though. Now I want my money."

"You . . . you shot White?" Clegg asked.

Suddenly he realized that if this was true, he would be all right. White was the key man. With him gone, Alred and the others would help. All Clegg needed to do now was to hire a new crew and he could still take care of Jim Baron.

"Yes, I shot White," Dillon said. "I should have started with him. Pete would be alive if I had. We ran into White in Texas when he called himself Keno Ross and I was calling myself Carstairs. I suppose he's had half a dozen names like I have. In my business it doesn't pay to keep the same name. Now that you savvy the deal, will you get me my dinero?"

Clegg got to his feet. He caught the edge of the table. For a moment he was dizzy. The whiskey, he told himself, or maybe it was just knowing that suddenly his future had cleared up. Dillon was right about one thing. They should have started with White.

He crossed the room to his office, the dizziness leaving him once that he was on his feet and walking. He opened the safe and took out both envelopes containing the greenbacks. As he counted out $1500 from the envelope that held his money and slipped it into the other one that had Alred's $500, his mind was already racing ahead into the afternoon.

A few hours! That was all he needed. He'd go to the Rafter A and Alred would get his crew together along with the other members of the Association; they'd ride down the Slow Water and finish the job that only a few minutes before had seemed impossible. One man, Jeremy White, made the difference.

He turned and started to leave the office. He didn't know that Dillon had followed him, but now Dillon stood only a few feet from him, an ugly, short-barreled gun in his hand.

Clegg cried out, "No, no. Here's your money."

The gun roared once. Clegg staggered back and bumped into the desk and sprawled across it. He rolled to the floor, feeling as if someone had hit him a crushing blow in the chest. Smiling, Dillon stooped and picked up the envelope.

"You won't be telling anybody what I just told you, my

friend," Dillon said. "It's my opinion Jim Baron will hang for killing you."

He left. Clegg put a hand to his chest and felt the blood, warm and sticky, and he knew he would not live long. Dillon was probably right about Jim Baron. He was alone in the mountains, but he could not prove he was there, so he would be blamed for the killing.

Clegg did not die at once. He held grimly to consciousness as he heard Dillon's horse gallop toward town. No pain. Just that crushing, heavy weight against his chest. He began to crawl across the office and into the front room, inch by inch, and then his strength was gone and he lay motionless.

Silence then, complete, absolute silence. The cook would come if he heard the shot, but the minutes passed and the cook did not come. Maybe he had left, too, without saying a word. Later, it seemed a long time later, he heard horses coming. He thought, *Alred, but he's too late.*

He was having trouble breathing. It would not be long now. The darkness was closing in around him.

26

Jim Baron woke before dawn. For a time he lay on his back, staring at the sky through the pine needles. Yesterday had been pleasant after Chick Lund and the other Skull riders had been started back downstream, pleasant just being lazy and having Carrie with him. Nora kept out of the way most of the time, which was fine, but it was not a situation that could be continued very long. The trouble was the girls probably didn't realize that.

The more he thought about it, the more he was convinced that they had to go back today. He didn't want Clegg or anyone else to think he was on the run. He had always gone on the principle that the only way to meet a problem was to stand up to it and face it, and to his way of thinking, the principle still held.

Too, he was concerned about Nora. For her own sake, she had to tell Sam Clegg she would not marry him, that he could not do anything to her or her father that would persuade her to change her mind.

As long as Nora ran away from Clegg, she would be afraid, but once she told him how she felt, she would conquer her fear. He guessed that was the trouble with Larry Bain and Buck Riley and everyone else in the country who knuckled down to Clegg. When you got right down to cases, he and Jeremy White were the only men in Slow Water County who understood that.

The sooner Clegg had this fact demonstrated, the better it would be for everyone. He considered going to see White. They had cooperated once and they could do it again, but now, watching the first hint of dawn appear over the eastern ridge, he decided that seeing White would have to wait. Right now it was more important to see Clegg. He might be riding into a hornet's nest, but he had a hunch that he had pulled their stingers when he had manhandled Chick Lund and had started the others on foot back down the creek without their pants and boots.

He got up and built a fire. He started coffee and sliced bacon and put it in the frying pan. A few minutes later Carrie sat up, sniffing audibly. "Are you hinting that we ought to get up?" she said.

"I'm not just hinting," he said, "I'm commanding."

"You think I'm a woman you can command?"

"No, but I'll tell you one thing. If you want any breakfast, you'll get up."

Carrie sighed resignedly. "Get up, Nora. The master is commanding."

"Sounds more like he's blackmailing us," Nora said.

Later, after they finished eating, Jim said, "We're going back. Nora, we'll stop at Skull before we ride into town. If his boys ain't there, and if he ain't heard what happened to 'em, I aim to tell him. Besides, you've got to tell Sam to his face that you won't marry him."

She stared at the ground, and began to tremble. "I'm afraid to go there, Jim. He'll make me stay."

"No he won't," Jim said. "I'll see he don't."

She looked up defiantly. "He'll kill you. I know how he feels about you. It's crazy to go to Skull. You'll be committing suicide."

He shook his head at her, grinning. "I may be crazy, but I sure don't figure on committing suicide."

"Jim's right," Carrie said gravely. "We talked about it yesterday, Nora. I don't think many of Dad's men will be at Skull. The bunch that were with Chick Lund will go to town to see Doc Ashton. They'll be afraid to face Dad. Jim may have to settle with Lund, but it won't be at Skull. Not for a while, anyhow. I know how Dad deals with his men. They're afraid of him just like a lot of other people."

Nora remained silent, her gaze still on the ground. Carrie went on, "I guess I know Sam Clegg better than anyone else. He's arrogant and proud and selfish and greedy, but there's a lot of bluff in him, too. Jim's the only one who ever called his bluff."

"And Jeremy White," Jim said.

She shrugged. "I don't know anything about Jeremy White, but I have a hunch he's worse than Dad."

Nora looked up, her face pale, a pulse pounding in her temples. "All right, I'll go to Skull with you. I . . . I hope you're right."

Jim got up. "I'll saddle up while you pack. We'll take most of the grub back to the store."

As he saddled the horses, Jim thought about Nora Bain and how she was showing her courage in agreeing to stop at Skull. Few people could rise above the kind of paralyzing fear that Sam Clegg aroused in Nora. He admired anyone who could.

The sun was up by the time they mounted and started downstream. They reached the mouth of the canyon and climbed to the top of the ridge that separated the forks of the Slow Water, Jim deciding that he would not stop at the B-in-a-Box until after he had seen Clegg. Going to Skull was the last thing Clegg would expect, and the sooner he was defied to his face, the better.

When they reached the valley of the South Fork and came in sight of the Skull buildings, they saw a man rush out of the house and mount his horse and head for Wheatridge on the run. At this distance Jim was not sure of the man's identity, but he looked like R. C. Dillon. Jim wondered about that. Dillon had said he would be staying at Skull, but why would he leave like this?

Jim glanced at Carrie who nodded. She said, "Let's get to the house in a hurry."

"Who was that man?" Nora asked.

"He was a stranger to me," Carrie said.

They touched up their horses, Jim not saying anything about it being Dillon because he wasn't sure. He was a stranger to both girls and the chances were neither had ever heard of him. They reached the house and dismounted, Carrie running on ahead. The moment she reached the front door, she screamed, "Jim."

He looked over her shoulder and saw Sam Clegg lying on his belly in the middle of the front room. A smear of blood was a stain on the floor all the way back to his office. He had been shot there, Jim thought, and by sheer will had dragged himself this far.

Carrie knelt on one side of him, Jim on the other. Carrie said, "Pa, it's Carrie. Can you hear me?"

He didn't say anything for a moment, but his fingers moved as if he were still trying to crawl. Jim turned him over and felt for his pulse. He had been shot in the chest, and although he was still alive, Jim doubted that he would live more than a few minutes.

"Dillon . . . shot . . . me," Clegg whispered.

Jim looked at Carrie. "I thought that's who it was, but I wasn't sure as far away as we were."

"I never heard of a man by that name," Carrie said. "Who is he?"

"He's an agent for a land development company who came up on the stage with me from Cheyenne," Jim answered. "At least that's what he claimed he was."

"Killer," Clegg breathed. "Murdered . . . Bean . . . White. Came . . . here . . . for his money."

"Why did he shoot you?" Carrie asked.

"He . . . told . . . too . . . much." Clegg seemed to stop breathing and Jim thought he was gone, then he said, "Told . . . me . . . they'd . . . lay . . . this onto . . . you."

Jim took a long breath, wondering if it was true about Jeremy White being dead, or had Clegg in his delirium after being shot imagined it? White was the man who had made the settlers fight and therefore stood in Clegg's way, so Clegg had wanted him dead.

"Nora," Clegg whispered. "Nora."

Jim rose and moved back, motioning for Nora to come to Clegg's side. She hesitated, glancing uneasily at Carrie, then she dropped to her knees beside the dying man. She said, "I'm here, Sam."

"New will," Clegg said, his tone so low that Nora had

to put her ear close to his mouth to hear. "Everything's . . . yours. Land . . . cattle . . . money."

Startled, Nora raised her head and looked at Carrie. "You hear that?" Carrie shook her head and Nora said, "He told me a new will left everything to me. That's . . . that's terrible. It can't be."

Jim, watching Carrie, was surprised to see the quick smile that touched her lips. "I'm glad, Nora. I hate Skull. I want no part of it."

"But . . . but . . ." Nora began.

"Jim," Carrie interrupted, "would you move him into his bedroom?"

"Sure," he said.

Picking the big man up, he carried him into his room and laid him on the bed. "Carrie, I'm going to town. Dillon won't stay there. Nobody in town will know what happened, so he'll get away. I'll tell Riley, and if he won't get Dillon or doesn't believe me, I'll take him."

"All right," she said. "I'll look after the pack horse. You'd better get started or he'll be gone."

"You want me to send Doc Ashton out?"

"I guess so. He won't do any good, but you'd better have him come." She looked at him, her eyes showing her worry, then she said, "Watch out for Chick Lund. He'll get out of bed to kill you if he knows you're in town."

"Then I'll tell him myself," Jim said.

He left the house and, mounting, took the road to Wheatridge, keeping his buckskin at a fast pace. He knew now that R. C. Dillon, not Pete Hammer, was the assassin, but no one in town knew that.

27

When Jim reached Wheatridge, he saw that the towns-men were gathered in little knots on the street talking in hushed tones. He wondered what had happened because they could not possibly have heard about Sam Clegg being shot.

Buck Riley was standing with Doc Ashton and Larry Bain in front of the Mercantile. Jim reined toward them and dismounted. As he tied, Riley stepped off the board-walk and moved to him. He said, "We brought Rose's body in as soon as Bones Porter told us what happened. I'm sorry, Jim. I know how it's been with you two, her being a mother and sister to you."

"Rose?" Jim forgot about Sam Clegg for the moment. "What's happened to Rose?"

"I guess you haven't heard," Riley said.

He told Jim what had happened, adding, "At least that's the way Bones Porter tells it. The ones who were with him backed him up, so it's probably straight. Red Schone's dead, all right. I don't think Porter would have shot him if the story wasn't true. I mean, it would take something like that. They've quit Skull. That other bunch you set afoot are all holed up in the hotel with sore feet."

Ashton had moved off the boardwalk, too. He said, "You ought to see their feet, Jim. Like raw beefsteak. They won't be riding for Sam or anybody else for a while. They can't even get their boots on." He shrugged his shoulders. "You know Sam must be just about alone out there on Skull."

The remark reminded Jim of why he was here. He turned to Riley. "Sam's dying. He was alive when I left Skull, but he has been shot in the chest, and I doubt he's alive now."

Larry Bain came up in time to hear what Jim said.

The three men stood as if frozen, eyes on Jim. They didn't say anything. They simply stood there in the hot, midday sunshine, staring at Jim. It occurred to him that if he had told them God no longer existed, they would not have been as shocked as they were now.

Finally Riley asked, "Who done it? You?"

Jim shook his head. "The girls and me stopped at Skull. I figured I'd shoot him if he jumped me, but he was on the floor when we got there. This stranger who calls himself R. C. Dillon done it. We seen him ride away as we came up. Sam was able to talk a little. He named Dillon."

Riley shook his head. "Dillon's a stranger. He wouldn't have no reason to beef Sam. Maybe you done it and you're laying it onto Dillon."

"I didn't shoot him," Jim said sharply. "You ought to know me well enough to be damned sure I'd admit it if I had. Carrie and Nora heard Sam name Dillon. He was the assassin the Association hired. Sam claims he killed Bean and White. Is White dead?"

"He's dead, all right," Riley said, "but it was his wife who shot him. Somebody killed the boy early this morning. That's what we were talking about when you rode up."

"Tad?" Jim asked. "Why? Nobody murders a boy of his age."

"Ed Majors thinks the killer mistook him for White in the thin light," Riley said. "Anyhow, Mrs. White blamed her husband for the boy's death, so she up and shot him. She turned herself in, but what in hell can I do with a woman who admits she murdered her husband?"

"You leave it to Judge Carr," Doc Ashton said. "I told you that."

"Yeah, I reckon so," Riley said uneasily. "My God, what's happening in this county? Everybody killing everybody else."

"What are you going to do about Dillon?" Jim asked. "Is he still in town?"

Riley nodded toward the livery stable. "He's over yonder arguing with Slim Evans about the price of a saddle horse. He couldn't find Slim for a while, and I wondered why he was in such a hurry. Maybe that answers my question."

"If you don't take him, I will," Jim said. "I told Carrie I would."

"I'll get him," Riley said, "and then I'll talk to Carrie and Nora just to be sure they heard what you did."

He turned and strode toward the livery stable, Ashton staring thoughtfully at his back. He said, "Nobody is going to waste many tears on Sam, least of all Buck. He's going to get up off his knees and he'll find out it's a real good feeling."

"We all will," Larry Bain said as if he were ashamed. "Some might have made it even if he had lived, but I'm not sure I would have."

"Carrie wants you to come out," Jim said to Ashton. "Sam will be dead before you get there, I think, but Carrie will feel better."

"Sure, I'll go," Ashton said. "Let's go saddle my horse. Might be Buck will need a little help with Dillon."

"Drygulchers are cowards," Jim said. "It won't be like facing a man who'll fight."

"You're probably right," Ashton said. "Let's go get my horse."

They were in the middle of the street when Ed Majors saw Jim and called to him. Jim and Ashton stopped until Ed reached them. As they stood waiting, Riley and Dillon came out of the livery stable, Riley's gun prodding Dillon in the back.

"I hope Dillon makes a run for it," Ashton said. "It'd save the county the cost of a trial."

Ed Majors was panting when he came up. He stopped and pulled in a long breath. "I had to tell you, Jim. You heard about Tad and Jeremy White?"

Jim nodded. "Buck was just telling me about it."

"I was staying at White's place," Ed said. "Some of the Skull riders came by and burned me out. Well, Mrs. White asked me to fetch her and Tad's body into town this morning. On the way she said she guessed she'd go to prison, but whether she did or not, she don't want to live on the farm. She says Simms and Wheeler won't stay there now that Jeremy's dead, so she wants to lease it to me and she promised to loan me enough money to get started on."

"Then you can send for your girl," Jim said.

Ed grinned. "I already have. I sent a wire the minute I had a chance to do it." He was trembling with excitement. He had to stop and swallow and then added in a rush of words, "I think I can make a living on the White place, a good living for my wife and me and all the kids we'll ever have."

"I know you can do it Ed, you just needed a good break," Jim told him.

Jim went on, leaving Ed smiling broadly. Ashton had already gone into the livery stable and now stood talking to Slim Evans who was saddling his horse. When Jim came up, Slim said, "For the first time since Buck was elected, he acted like a sheriff. I was sure glad to see him take that fellow Dillon out of here like he done."

"Baron."

Jim wheeled. Chick Lund stood in the archway, a gun in his hand. For a moment Jim was paralyzed, unable even to breathe. He was remembering that the last thing Carrie had said was to watch out for Chick Lund, but here he was, caught with his Colt in leather. Lund would gun him down the instant he started to draw.

"You think I was gonna let you beat hell out of me and forget it?" Lund asked. "I'm gonna kill you, Baron. I want you to think about it a while before I let you have it."

Jim, staring at Lund, saw that the man could barely stand erect. His battered face was a mass of purple bruises. His eyes held Jim's attention, eyes that were filled with a feral hate that Jim had never seen before in the eyes of any human being.

Jim knew he had a few seconds of life, no more, and he felt the keen injustice of it, that now when the problems that had faced him seemed solved and there was the promise of peace in Slow Water County, he would die this way, without a chance to defend himself. No use to beg, for Chick Lund must already have made the decision that he would willingly hang for the privilege of killing Jim Baron.

Slowly Lund raised his gun, the next second a gun roared from the street and Lund was spun around just as Doc Ashton yelled, "Look out behind you."

Jim dived toward a stall on one side of the runway and turned, drawing his gun as he made the turn. A gun from the other end of the runway crashed into Ashton's words, the bullet splintering the edge of the wall of the stall just above Jim's head. A second slug kicked up litter beside Jim, then he had his gun in his hand and he leveled it and fired.

It was Rufe Smith who had been standing at the other end of the runway, the Rufe Smith who had said up there on the North Fork that they'd get Jim, that by God they'd hang him sure. So they had tried, Chick from one end of the runway and Rufe Smith at the other.

It had been a dead-sure trap, both men hating Jim Baron so much for what he had done to them that they would pay any price to kill him. Or had they thought that Sam Clegg would get them off just as he had got men off in the past?

Jim told himself he would never know the answer to that question. He moved along the runway toward Smith who lay on his face in the straw and manure. Ashton came out of a stall, picked up Smith's right wrist and felt for the pulse and shook his head.

He said, "He's dead."

Jim wheeled and strode toward the archway. Ed Majors stood holding his gun on Lund who was very much alive. He had a bullet-smashed right arm. When Ashton reached him, he said, "We'll take him to my office and patch that arm up and then Riley can jail him for attempted murder."

"Thanks, Ed," Jim said. "They damned near had me."

Ed grinned. "I wanted to pay back a little of what I

owe you. Besides, I always like to see a man have an even break and they sure didn't aim to give you one."

"They didn't for a fact," Jim agreed. "What do you mean, pay me back. You don't owe me nothing."

Ed holstered his gun. He said gravely, "I owe you more'n you'll ever know, son."

And Ashton, who had hold of Lund's good arm, nodded and added, "That's right, Jim. All of us owe you more than you know." He motioned toward Jim's horse. "Go on back to Skull. Tell Carrie I'll be along in a few minutes."

Jim walked to his buckskin, untied him, and mounted. As he turned his horse and rode out of town, he saw Buck Riley leave the courthouse. Jim had never seen him stand as tall and straight as he did now. It was, as Larry Bain had said, a good feeling for Riley to get off his knees, and for all the rest of them, too.

Now, looking out across the rolling, grass-covered prairie, it occurred to Jim that it was a good feeling just to be alive.